Jarvis C. Archer was one of those "Big I—Little You" types.

He came to see me, Donald Lam, because he wanted to hire a man-woman team of private eyes to keep a twenty-four-hour-a-day guard on his secretary. To Bertha Cool he explained it this way:

"I want to find out who is annoying my secretary and I want this annoyance stopped. I want adequate measures taken to see that this thing is nipped in the bud."

"The bud's become a blossom," Bertha commented acidly. "And if you're personally trying to tell us she's nothing to you other than a secretary, you must have a poor opinion of our intelligence."

"I am not accustomed to having my word questioned, Mrs. Cool."

"Then you'd better get a more convincing line. And leave us four hundred dollars in cash. That'll cover two days and expenses. If we haven't got a result, you can then put up some more money or let us go."

And that's how Donald Lam and Bertha Cool got mixed up in a murder and a whirlwind of action which Erle Stanley Gardner, writing under his pseudonym A. A. Fair, tells about in **FISH OR CUT** ~~published by~~ ~~company.~~

Also by A. A. Fair

Bachelors Get Lonely
The Bigger They Come
Kept Women Can't Quit
Pass the Gravy
Shills Can't Cash Chips
Some Slips Don't Show
Try Anything Once
You Can Die Laughing

Published by Pocket Books, Inc.

Are there paperbound books you want but cannot find at your retail stores?

You can get any title that is in print in these famous series:
Pocket Book editions • Pocket *Cardinal* editions • Permabook editions
The Pocket Library • Washington Square Press • All Saints Press
Simply enclose retail price plus 10¢ per book
for mailing and handling costs.
Not responsible for orders containing cash.
Please send check or money order to:
Mail Service Department
Pocket Books, Inc.
1 West 39th Street
New York, N.Y. 10018

Free catalogue sent on request

FISH
OR CUT
BAIT

A. A. FAIR

(Erle Stanley Gardner)

PUBLISHED BY POCKET BOOKS, INC. NEW YORK

FISH OR CUT BAIT

William Morrow edition published April, 1963
A Pocket Book edition
1st printing .... October, 1964

L

Chapter 1

THE MAN whom Elsie Brand ushered into my private office was one of the "Big I-Little You" type of executives.

"This is Mr. Donald Lam," Elsie said, and then to me, "Mr. Jarvis C. Archer, Mr. Lam."

He gave me a firm handclasp, with just a trifle more emphasis than was necessary at the last. I rather suspected these final few ounces of pressure were for the purpose of indicating to me that his executive mind had sized up the situation, had reached a decision and that he was now prepared to go ahead.

He was somewhere in his late thirties, with steely gray eyes, rather heavy, dark eyebrows, dark hair, a high forehead, broad shoulders and a developing paunch which he tried to hold in during our talk, as though he had been practicing posture in front of a full-length mirror. He had probably practiced everything he did in front of a mirror—he was that type.

"Mr. Lam," he said, "I have heard a great deal about you and about your firm."

I nodded.

"A matter of extreme delicacy has come up," he said, "and I find myself in need of the services of a detective agency, an agency composed of both a woman and a man. Therefore, I have decided to consult with you."

"I see," I said noncommittally.

"I won't mention names," he said, "but I have talked with a business executive for whom you did some work. He was lavish in his praise. I have, however, been less fortunate in finding out about your partner, B. Cool. The 'B' I understand stands for Bertha."

"That's right."

"Can you describe her to me?"

"No."

"What?" he asked in surprise.

I smiled and said, "Words can only do so much. You have to know Bertha to appreciate her. Shall I arrange an interview?"

"Not until I've discussed a few preliminaries with you," he said. "I take it, Bertha Cool is competent?"

"Highly competent."

"As a woman she is in a rather peculiar profession, one which at times may . . . well, may lead to physical jeopardy. Can Miss Cool take care of herself in a situation of that sort?"

"Mrs. Cool," I said, "can take care of any situation which may arise."

Archer looked me over thoughtfully. "I see," he said.

"Why do you need a team consisting of both a man and a woman?" I asked.

"I want to employ a bodyguard for a young woman. The bodyguard must be with her day and night. Naturally, it would be embarrassing to have a man on the night shift. On the other hand, the day shift *will* require a man."

Again Archer looked me over critically.

"How do you react to violence, Mr. Lam?" he asked.

"I try to avoid it."

"You hardly have the build that one would associate with a detective."

"That's right," I agreed wearily. "And since it's quite apparent that you want physical protection for the young woman you mention, you had probably better look elsewhere."

"Now, wait a minute, wait a minute," he said. "I didn't say that at all, and I don't want you putting words in my mouth. The situation is very peculiar. In fact, it's somewhat unique. There *may* be an element of danger involved, but I understand that you're cool as a cucumber when it comes to facing danger. You have the reputation of being able to think your way out of trouble."

"You'd better take what you've heard," I told him, "and divide it by two. In the meantime, if you want to discuss

6

the matter with Mrs. Cool, I'll try and get her before she leaves the office. She's going out on an appointment in a few minutes."

"Very well," he said. "I'd like to talk with both of you."

I picked up the phone and had the operator put through the call to Bertha's office.

"*Now* what is it?" Bertha said, when she recognized my voice on the line.

I said, "A Mr. Jarvis C. Archer is in the office. He wants to arrange a bodyguard service, a day and night operation. You on nights, me on days."

"Nuts to that stuff," Bertha said. "A twelve-hour day? What does he think he's doing, running a sweat shop? Tell him to go to hell."

I said, "He came to us because the person to be guarded is a young woman, and he would like to secure the services of people of both sexes, the woman for night duty and the man for day duty."

"And because your firm was highly recommended," Archer suggested to me as an interpolation.

"Now, wait a minute," Bertha said. "Have you discussed compensation with this guy?"

"No."

"Then don't," Bertha snapped. "You're a push-over for a hard luck story. You pilot him in here and let me soften him up."

"You had an appointment this morning, I believe," I suggested.

"Only with that goddam dentist," Bertha said, "and he can wait for a little while, if he has to. Bring that guy in here."

I hung up the phone and said, "Mrs. Cool is leaving on an important appointment, but she can see you rather briefly, if you're prepared to come with me immediately."

"Let's go," he said.

I escorted him out of my private office, across the reception room and into Bertha Cool's private office.

Bertha, one hundred and sixty-five pounds of belligerence, somewhere around sixty, with a form like a roll of barbed

7

wire, looked up from the creaky swivel chair with eyes that were as hard as the diamonds on her hands.

"Mr. Archer, Mrs. Cool," I said.

"Hello, Archer," Bertha said. "Sit down. You've got about five minutes. Tell me what's on your mind—fast."

Archer wasn't accustomed to having people assume the conversational initiative with him. He tried to suck in his stomach another inch or two and looked down at Bertha seated there at the desk in the creaky swivel chair, with a look that was designed to let her know he was the one who gave the orders.

His gaze locked with hers and then wavered. He went over and sat down.

"Shoot," Bertha said.

Archer said, "Here is one of my cards. I am an executive with the Molybdenum Steel Research Importing Company. Under no circumstances is my identity to be disclosed, or the fact that any executive of the Molybdenum Steel Company has any connection with the case."

"What's the woman's name?" Bertha snapped at him, looking at her wrist watch.

"The young woman is my confidential secretary. She is a very valuable secretary and I would hate to lose her. But unless this situation can be handled, and handled at once, I am going to lose her services."

"What's her name?" Bertha repeated.

"Marilyn Chelan."

"Where does she live?"

"In an apartment house not too far from our place of business. But I think perhaps you're getting a false impression, Mrs. Cool."

"In what way?"

"You seem to feel that there may be some personal interest. This is a business matter."

"What do you want?"

"Miss Chelan has been getting threatening letters through the mail. She has been subjected to repeated annoyance. People ring her telephone at all hours of the night. She picks up the instrument and can hear someone at the other end of the line breathing heavily, then the person hangs up. It is rapidly giving Miss Chelan a nervous breakdown."

"What does this person want?" Bertha asked.

"Apparently nothing."

"See the postal authorities!" Bertha snapped, watching Archer like a hawk. "They can do more than a private agency with threatening letters."

"We have hesitated to enlist the aid of the postal authorities because of a desire to avoid publicity."

"Getting an unlisted telephone number?" Bertha asked.

"We've done that twice. It does no good. The calls continue on the unlisted number as soon as it is assigned."

"Put a shut-off on the telephone bell so it can only ring at certain times," Bertha said.

"We hesitate to do that," Archer told her, "because Miss Chelan has a mother in Salt Lake City who is not in good health. She wants to be able to keep in touch with her mother by phone."

"All right," Bertha said, looking at her watch, "my time's about up. What *do* you want?"

"I would like to have you and your partner work in alternate shifts. You working nights, of course, and Mr. Lam working daytimes."

"No third party?"

"No third party," he said. "I want this kept in the high executive level of your firm."

"That would mean a twelve-hour day," Bertha pointed out.

"My mathematics are quite adequate to divide twenty-four by two," he said.

"What I'm getting at," Bertha told him, "is that all this would run into overtime."

"I would assume so."

"The company is going to pay?" Bertha asked.

He said hastily, "That doesn't need to concern your agency. You will bill Marilyn Chelan for your services. I will personally guarantee your bill."

"Nobody's going to guarantee anything," Bertha said. "On

9

a deal of that sort, we work on a cash basis. A hundred and fifty dollars a day, plus expenses."

"Isn't that rather steep?" Archer asked.

"Hell, no," Bertha told him. "That's cheap. I started to say two hundred a day. When you consider a twelve-hour day, it's a man-killing job."

"Very well," Archer said. "A hundred and fifty a day."

"All right," Bertha said. "What's the pitch?"

"I want to find out who is causing this annoyance. I want the annoyance stopped. I want adequate measures taken to see that this thing is nipped in the bud."

"The bud's become a blossom," Bertha said. "And if you're personally trying to tell us you're going to pay a hundred and fifty bucks a day just to keep your secretary from being annoyed, and she's nothing to you other than a secretary, you must have a poor opinion of our intelligence."

Archer said, "I am not accustomed to having my word questioned, Mrs. Cool."

"Better get a more convincing line, then," Bertha snapped.

"What I said was that I would personally guarantee the payment and that I didn't want the company mentioned. I didn't say I wouldn't reimburse myself from the company."

I said, "Let's get one thing straight. No matter who pays the bill, we have to have one client and be loyal to that client. In this case, you're hiring us but we are protecting Marilyn Chelan. We're doing everything necessary to protect her. She's the *only* one we're protecting."

"That's the way I want it," Archer said. "That is what I have been trying to tell you. I am concerned about her. You are to protect her."

"All right," Bertha said. "On a deal of that sort, we don't want guarantees and credit is no good. You leave us four hundred dollars spot cash. That will cover two days and expenses. If we haven't got a result at the end of two days, you can put up some more money, or let us go.

"Now then," she went on, before Archer could protest, "when we find the person who's doing this, what do you want us to do?"

"Do whatever is necessary to stop it," Archer said, "but

10

do it without any publicity. There must be no publicity at all."

Bertha said, "Well, I can make a pretty good guess right now what's back of all this. You've either been making a play for this babe, or she's making a play for you, and someone else in the office who doesn't like to see that situation develop is doing something about it."

"That is the obvious explanation," Archer said with frosty dignity. "If I thought it was the true one, I wouldn't be here."

"You married?" Bertha asked.

"Yes. And that doesn't enter into the picture."

"How do you know it doesn't?"

"I know. You can take my word for it."

"Why is this girl so valuable?" Bertha asked suspiciously.

"She knows my work. She gets along well with everyone. She has a photographic memory for faces. She never forgets a face, a name or a connection. I am somewhat inclined to be the other way. Many times I can't recall either the face or name of some of our contacts.

"Miss Chelan would make an absolutely invaluable secretary for a politician. Even in my work, her ability to remember names and faces is so uncanny that it is of the greatest value."

"How long has she been with you?" I asked.

"About eight months."

"How long with the firm?"

"The same length of time."

"What about her background?"

"I don't know much about it. She came here from Salt Lake City, registered with the employment agency that handles our personnel, and as I was in need of a secretary, they sent her to me for a tryout. I found her unusually competent and gave her a week's trial. It was then I learned of her remarkable ability to remember* faces and names—qualities which are invaluable in our work."

"You've never been to her apartment?" Bertha asked.

"I didn't say that," Archer said. "I have been there in a business way, yes. . . . I have had to go there to talk this matter over with her. This is hardly a problem one would

11

discuss in the office, particularly with a business that works in areas as sensitive as our business."

"Just what is your business?" Bertha asked. "This card says Molybdenum Steel Research Importing Company. Now, that doesn't mean a damned thing to me."

"It doesn't have to," Archer said, getting to his feet and pulling out a roll from which he took four one-hundred-dollar bills. "If you'll kindly give me a receipt, Mrs. Cool, I'll give you Miss Chelan's address and you can go up and start work at once. That is, Mr. Lam can take on the day shift and you can be prepared to go on duty starting to-night."

"Wait a minute," Bertha said, looking up from the receipt she was signing. "If she's employed as your secretary, she'll be working during the daytime."

"She's on a temporary layoff until we can get this thing straightened out," Archer said.

"She's at the Neddler Arms on Neddler Drive. Her apartment is 617. I don't have her telephone number. It's an unlisted telephone and the number has been changed lately, so you'll just have to go out there and explain the situation to her. Mr. Lam can simply tell her that I have retained your firm. She will understand, because we have discussed the situation."

Archer pulled in his stomach, buttoned his coat, bowed from the hips, said, "I think you can get any other information from Miss Chelan. *You're* in a hurry and *my* time is valuable—*very* valuable."

Archer walked out of the office.

Bertha looked at me and said, "The sonofabitch—trying to pretend that he isn't the sugar daddy!"

I didn't say anything.

Bertha sighed. "You feel like screaming at him, 'Quit holding your breath and let your belly down where it belongs!' After a man gets past thirty-five and starts putting on weight, trying to impress people that he's got the figure he used to have at twenty-two is strictly a losing proposition.

"All right, Donald, you'll have to get that moon-eyed secretary of yours briefed on what's going on. I'll handle things at

12

the office during the day for the next few days. I'll show up at nine o'clock tonight to take over."

"Nine o'clock?"

"That's the way we'll work," she said, "nine to nine. And remember, we only have a hundred-buck margin for expenses, so when it comes to dinners, let *her* pick up the tab."

"We have a hundred dollars for two days," I said. "We could afford to—"

"There you go!" Bertha said. "Giving away all the profits. Let *her* buy the dinners or stay home and cook them."

"You're late for your dental appointment," I reminded her.

"No, I'm not," she said. "I don't have to be up there for fifteen minutes. I always lie to the office about the time of my appointments. That gives me a fifteen-minute cushion. Otherwise, I'd never get anywhere on time, and that damned dentist has a snippy office nurse who charges you for the doctor's time the minute he's ready for you—and if you aren't there, it's just too bad. If he wasn't such a good dentist, I'd flatten that snippy office nurse into a grease spot."

Bertha sighed. "So now we've got ourselves a job, baby-sitting!"

She heaved herself up out of the creaky swivel chair, strode to the door, turned and said, "And don't make any passes at this babe. That Archer guy strikes me as a guy who could get crazy jealous."

Chapter 2

THE YOUNG WOMAN who answered my ring at Apartment 617 was about twenty-seven, blond, blue-eyed, with a nice figure and a look of intelligence on her face. But her eyes were the eyes of a hunted, frightened animal.

"Miss Chelan?" I asked.

"Yes," she said cautiously.

13

"I'm Donald Lam of the firm of Cool and Lam. We have been retained to act as bodyguards for you."

"Oh, yes," she said.

"You know about it?" I asked.

She stood in the doorway. "May I see your credentials, please?"

I took my credentials from my pocket. She checked them carefully, then smiled. "Won't you come in, Mr. Lam?"

It was a nice apartment. Although there was a wall bed in the living room, I was sure it was a two-room apartment with a kitchenette.

"You'll forgive me for being so cautious," she said, "but I've had a whole series of annoying experiences."

"I know," I told her.

"I had expected a more . . . well, a more— Well, a heavier type."

I said, "Have you been subjected to physical annoyance or mental annoyance?"

"Mental."

I didn't say anything more, and, after a moment, she laughed nervously and said, "You have an interesting way of making a point.

"Won't you please sit down, Mr. Lam, You're going to have to make yourself at home here. And, since we're going to be together a great deal of the time, you may as well call me Marilyn and I'll call you Donald.

"Another one of those things just came in by special delivery, and I confess that I'm a little upset."

"What do you mean by 'those things'?" I asked.

"This one's on the table there. You may look at it."

"That special delivery letter?"

"Yes."

I took a pair of tweezers and some gloves from my brief case and picked it up.

"Why the tweezers and gloves?" she asked.

"I don't want to damage any fingerprints that are on it, so I'm holding it by the edges, so far as possible, and I don't want to leave my fingerprints on it."

"You can't get fingerprints from paper."

14

"You seem to speak with the tone of authority. Have you consulted the police?"

"No, but Mr. Archer says that you can't get fingerprints from paper. Only occasionally will there be enough of a print to be developed in iodine vapors, and he says it's not worth while trying to get fingerprints from paper."

I took the paper from the envelope and unfolded it, holding it by the edges.

It had been pasted together from lines cut from newspapers. It said: GET OUT, GET OUT, GET OUT WHILE THERE IS YET TIME. WE MEAN BUSINESS. THERE ARE CERTAIN THINGS YOU WOULDN'T LIKE TO HAVE THE PUBLIC KNOW ABOUT. GET OUT.

I carefully folded the letter, put it back in the envelope and inspected the address.

The name Miss Marilyn Chelan, and the address, Apartment 617 Neddler Arms Apartments, Neddler Drive, City, had been put on with a rubber stamp, apparently made from one of those toy printing presses which are sold for kids at Christmas. It was a hand stamp and the right-hand side was a little lighter than the left.

"That's the tenth," she said.

"All the same?"

"Just about."

"What have you done with them?"

"I'm saving them. Mr. Archer thinks I should burn them, but— Well, if the thing gets bad enough, *I'm* going to go to the postal authorities, regardless of what *anyone* says."

"What do you mean, bad enough?"

"I don't know—worse."

"How much worse?"

"As far as I'm concerned, things couldn't get *any* worse. I'm a nervous wreck. They've given me two weeks' leave of absence at the office. Of course, the people up there don't know what it is. They think I'm ill."

"Where's the office?"

She looked at me with sudden suspicion. "You should know."

"I just wanted to check. It's my turn now."

15

"Well, you don't need to check on things like that."

"What else?" I asked. "What other threats?"

"All just about the same," she said.

"Threats to bring some information to light that you wouldn't want to have generally known?"

She was silent.

"Anything in your past?" I asked.

"I think everyone has something in his or her past that— Well, something . . ."

As her voice trailed into silence, I said, "What about the telephone calls?"

"They come in spurts," she said. "There will be four or five of them in an hour, then I won't get any for a long time. Then perhaps two or three."

"And what are the phone calls, the same thing as the letters you get?"

"No, those phone calls are different. The phone rings, I pick it up to answer, and I can hear someone breathing heavily."

"Man or woman?"

"Heavens, I can't tell. It sounds like a great big burly man, the way he breathes, but it *could* be a woman putting on an act."

"And then what happens?"

"The person at the other end of the line hangs on until I hang up."

"Says something?"

"Never."

"How well do you know Jarvis Archer?"

"He's my boss."

"How well do you know Jarvis Archer?"

"I'm his secretary. I've worked for him for nearly a year."

"How well do you know Jarvis Archer?"

She met my eyes defiantly. "Is this catechism in accordance with your instructions?"

"My instructions were to find out who was doing all this and put a stop to it. You want that, don't you?"

"Yes."

16

"How well do you know Jarvis Archer?"

"Well."

"He's married?"

"Yes."

"He's been here in the apartment?"

"Some."

"He's listened to those telephone calls?"

She hesitated a moment, then shook her head and said, "No."

"Why not?"

"He hasn't been here often and there haven't been that number of calls. As I told you, they go in a series."

I said, "The main thing to do when the next phone call comes in is to make the person show his hand—or her hand. You think it could be a jealous wife?"

"I don't know who it is."

"You just hang on to the phone and say nothing?"

"Most of the time I just get numb with terror. At first I tried to talk. I don't say much now."

I said, "After this, try to make conversation. Try and say something that will make him—or her—talk."

"But how could I—"

The phone rang.

She jumped at the sound of the phone as though someone had stuck her with a pin. Automatically, she reached forward to answer it, then her hand was stopped in mid-motion. She looked at me with panic-stricken eyes. "That may be one now," she said.

"See if it is," I said.

The phone rang again.

She said, "Oh, I hope not, I hope not. We've just had the number changed—a *new* unlisted number. I hoped that that would put a stop to these phone calls."

Again the phone rang.

I pointed to it.

She picked it up, said, "Hello," and then her face set in lines of terror. She looked at me and nodded.

I reached over her shoulder, took the instrument from her

17

hand and placed it to my ear. I could hear heavy, ominous breathing.

I said, "Hello, fourflusher. This is Donald Lam talking. In case you don't know who I am, you'll find out after a while. I'm the guy that's going to track you down and send you to prison."

I quit talking.

The heavy breathing continued.

"You want to know why I've called you a fourflusher," I said into the phone casually. "Well, that's because you're a piker, a quitter, a two-bit jerk. You make a lot of big threats and you don't do anything about them. You ring up on the telephone and breathe heavily."

I laughed. "You're going to have to do better than that from now on," I said. "What else have you got to offer?"

There was no sound except the heavy breathing.

I said, "With these dial telephones, it's a little difficult to trace a call, but it's not impossible. And when we nab you, you're going to have a nice, long stay in a federal penitentiary. Using the mails for illegal purposes, blackmail, attempted extortion— Oh, we can give you quite a ride.

"Also," I went on, "you've made a mistake with that last missive you sent. You got your finger in paste and left a very nice little fingerprint for us. How do you like that?"

I stopped talking, and the phone was hung up at the other end of the line.

I put the receiver back into place.

"What happened?" she asked.

"He hung up."

"*He* hung up?"

"Whoever it was at the other end of the line."

"Why," she said, "that's the first time that's ever happened. Usually, they stay right on there until *I* hang up."

"Have you ever tried talking the way I did?"

"No, of course not. I wouldn't have the nerve. I've asked who is it and what they want and why on earth they keep annoying me and what have I ever done to them, and things of that sort, but I've never talked the way you did."

"And no answer?" I asked.

18

"No answer except the heavy breathing."

"Never heard a voice?"

"Never a voice."

"And you've had this unlisted number for how long?"

"This last one was only put in service about twenty-four hours ago, and it was handled most discreetly."

"You did it?"

"No, Mr. Archer worked through friends at the telephone company and every precaution was taken to see that the number was kept absolutely confidential. My mother and Mother's nurse are the only ones who know it—and Mother's doctor."

I said, "Well, I've been given a pretty fair demonstration. So far, we've had a phone call and a special delivery letter. . . . You haven't had any experience with knocks on the door at times when you couldn't go to the door, when you were taking a shower, or things of that sort?"

"No, nothing except the letters and the telephone calls."

I picked up the phone, called a recording company that did work for us and said, "I want a small portable tape recorder with a connection for telephone conversations. I want a good one that's sensitive, and I want a hook-up that will faithfully record every sound that comes over the telephone, and to hell with the federal regulations. Send it up to Apartment 617 at the Neddler Arms Apartments just as fast as you can, with a good supply of tape, and charge it to Cool and Lam."

I was assured a recorder would be on its way up within thirty minutes.

I hung up the phone and settled myself in a chair.

"There may be other calls," she said. "Sometimes there will be two or three within an hour or an hour and a half."

"Good," I said. "I like to talk with the guy, or, rather, I like to let him listen to me. So many people interrupt me when I'm talking."

"What's the tape recorder for?" she asked.

"I want to record the sound of the breathing."

"What do you mean?"

"People breathe in an individual way," I said. "When

19

you take a lie detector test, one of the things they check is your respiration. When you go to a hospital, they take your pulse and respiration.

"I want to find out whether your caller is breathing heavily into the telephone as an act, or whether it's just the nature of the critter."

"It is certainly heavy breathing," she said. "I think it's an act."

"I also think it's an act," I told her. "If it isn't an act, he's suffering from asthma or has a heart condition and has been climbing stairs in a hurry."

"I have an appointment with the hairdresser this afternoon," she said. "You're supposed to be my bodyguard. What do you do?"

"I go sit in the hairdressing establishment with you," I said.

"You stay with me *all* the time?"

"You're not out of our sight for a minute," I said.

"This is going to be . . . frightfully intimate."

"It's going to be frightfully intimate," I told her. "Ever been married?"

She hesitated a few moments, then said, "Yes."

I said, "All right, you can stand it, then. Just pretend I'm your husband."

She laughed nervously. "Do I have to go *that* far?"

I met her eyes. "No."

The tape recorder was delivered inside of forty minutes. We went to the beauty shop. I sat in a chair and watched Marilyn getting her hair shampooed and dried, her nails manicured. People in the beauty shop looked at me curiously. Most of them felt I was a new sugar daddy and appraised me accordingly.

When we got back to the apartment, I hooked up the tape recorder to the telephone and we were there about twenty minutes before the phone rang again, with another call.

Marilyn nodded to me, and I took over and hooked up the tape recorder.

"Well, hello," I said. "I hope we haven't inconvenienced

20

you by being out. Have you been calling while we were gone?"

The voice said nothing.

I said, "After thinking the matter over, I decided it was a lot better to go to the F.B.I. than it was to try and handle things ourselves. Of course, they told me not to say anything, but I felt that I'd give you fair warning. You're pretty much of an amateur, you know, and actually you're playing right into our hands."

I waited and listened to the breathing.

I said, "Tune in on your television and listen to the commercials. There are several that give you a good sinus drainage tablet and you can get over that wheezing. You sound like a peanut stand with a leaky valve.

"I suppose that's part of your act. You stand up in front of the mirror and look ferocious and breathe through your teeth, and think, 'My God, how I'm going to frighten that woman.' "

I laughed.

The breathing continued for a moment, then the phone was hung up at the other end.

"He hung up?" Marilyn asked, as she saw me put the receiver in place.

I nodded, but left the tape recorder on and dialed UL 3-1212, then waited.

After a few seconds, a feminine voice came over the line. "The time is five—seventeen— and ten seconds." There was a pause, then, "The time is five—seventeen—and twenty seconds . . ."

I cradled the telephone, switched off the tape recorder and set my watch.

"What's the idea?" Marilyn asked.

"Of the tape recorder?"

"No, of the time."

"I'm just checking," I said. "There may be something to be learned by studying the time element."

"I don't get it," she said.

I said, "That's routine police procedure. Whenever they have a series of burglaries, they stick pins on a map in the

21

locations of the burglaries. They use different colored pins for different hours of the day, and finally get a map where they can study the clusters of pins and tell something about the habits of the criminals."

"But I don't see how the time element is going to help here."

"It just gives a record," I said. "I also want a record of the breathing. . . . What do we do about dinner?"

"I take you out to dinner," she said. "I have expense money. Or would you prefer, for the sake of appearances, to have me give you the money and you pick up the tab?"

"You pay," I said, "and that way you can put it on your expense account instead of having it go on mine. My partner is sensitive to expense accounts. Now, she'll be here at nine o'clock and we should be back here at that time, or else arrange to have her join us where we're eating."

"Oh, I like to eat early," she said. "But this brings up . . . well, it brings up an embarrassing question. I want to shower and change."

"That's the bedroom?" I asked, nodding toward the door.
"Yes."

"And the bath is off that?"
"Yes."

"Any other exit out of the place?"
"No."

"You go ahead and shower," I said. "Leave the door open. I won't look. But I want it so I can hear you if you should scream, and I want to be where I can see that nobody climbs up the fire escape, slides in through a window and makes any passes."

"There's never been any trouble except with the special deliveries and the telephone calls," she said.

"Well, that doesn't mean that we can count on it," I told her. "I'm a bodyguard."

"I get it," she said. "I furnish the body, you furnish the guard."

"Something like that."

"Well, it's terribly intimate," she said, "but I guess— Frankly, once I get accustomed to it, I feel I'm going to like it that way. . . . I felt so alone and isolated, and now that you're here, I— Well, I have a feeling that you know what you're doing."

"Thanks."

"What kind of a woman is your partner? Will she be sympathetic?"

"No."

"She won't?" Marilyn asked in surprise.

I said, "Bertha doesn't go much for sympathy."

"What does she go for?"

"Action, efficiency and cash."

"How old is she?"

"Somewhere around sixty, perhaps fifty-five."

"Heavy?"

"Like a roll of barbed wire," I said.

"She's strong?"

"Like an ox."

"Donald, tell me, does she like you?"

"Sometimes I think she does," I said, "and sometimes I think she hates my guts. I irritate the hell out of her."

"Why do you do that, Donald?"

"Because," I said, "she thinks in a groove and I don't want to get dragged down into that groove."

"You make it sound interesting. I think I'm going to enjoy this. I'm feeling a lot better already."

"Go ahead and take your shower," I told her.

Fifteen minutes later, the phone started ringing.

"How about it?" I asked. "Do you want me to answer it?"

"Heavens, no," she called. "If it's my mother and a man's voice answers, I'd be— Well, I'd have a lot of explaining to do. Just hold on and I'll answer it."

The phone kept ringing. I heard the sound of bare feet, then she glided past me with nothing on except a towel which had been hastily looped around her body just under the arms. She was struggling with her right hand, holding it in place. She picked up the telephone with her left hand.

She said, "Hello," then I saw her stiffen. She nodded to me.

I moved over, and she handed me the instrument.

I switched on the tape recorder.

23

The breathing was heavy at the other end of the line. There was no other sound.

I said, "Well, you're working fast today, aren't you? How's your sinus? I can see that what I said before stung you to the quick and you wanted to get revenge. But you haven't got guts enough to come out and face the situation, so you're pulling this cheap, amateurish telephone stunt again."

Marilyn Chelan stood there completely fascinated, forgetful of her lack of attire, listening, watching the spools on the tape recorder revolve.

I had the tape recorder in the monitoring position so that she could hear everything that was coming over the telephone as it was being recorded.

I said, "It's one thing to frighten women with a lot of this kid stuff, but it's entirely different when you're up against a man. Why don't you come out in the open, you cowardly rat? Or are you perhaps a woman, one of the frustrated kind that never had the opportunity to lead a normal life, never appealed to any man worthy of the name, and so are insanely jealous of anyone who has any normal sex appeal.

"You're one or the other, you—"

A man's voice came over the line. "You smart-aleck sonofabitch! Before I get done with you, I'll—"

The phone slammed at the other end of the line.

I dialed the number for the time signal.

The voice of the girl said, "The time is six—oh-five—and *forty* seconds . . . The time is six—oh-five—and *fifty* seconds . . ."

I hung up and cut off the tape recorder.

"All right, Marilyn," I said, "we know it's a man, and we know he's vulnerable. He can't take too much needling."

She stood there looking at me with large, round eyes.

"Donald," she said, "I think you're wonderful, simply wonderful!"

Then suddenly she became conscious of the gap in the towel, grabbed it with her hand and said, "Heavens!" and dashed back into the bedroom.

24

I checked my watch with the time that had come over the tape and found I was within a couple of seconds.

We went out to dinner, got back about eight-forty-five, and there was a special delivery letter.

I held it up to the light and could see that it was another threatening letter composed of segments from newspaper headlines and pasted together on a sheet of paper.

"This one," I said, "we're not going to open."

"Not open?" she asked. "Why?"

"Why should we? You know what's in it."

"I know, but I like to see what— And perhaps you could get a clue. . . ."

"No," I said. "When this thing comes to a head, we'll get this fellow for using the mail to send threatening letters. If we open the envelope, there's nothing to stop him from claiming that we sent an envelope through the mail and put our own threatening message in it, in order to frame him. We'll leave this one just the way it was sent through the mail, sealed, stamped and addressed, with the cancellation mark on the stamp and on the special delivery stamp, and then we'll let the district attorney hand it to the jury unopened, then let one of the jurors open it and read the message.

"That's the best way to prove that something was sent through the mail."

"Donald, you're . . . you're simply great!"

"Wait until I've done something other than routine," I said.

A few minutes later, there was a ring at the bell.

"Another special delivery?" I asked.

The bell rang a long and two shorts.

"Oh, it's Mr. Archer," she said, and dashed to the door and opened it.

"Oh, Mr. Archer, we're really getting someplace. I think we're doing some good. Donald has installed a tape recorder and he needled the person on the other end into talking. It's the first time we've heard a voice. Now we know it's a man and not a woman."

Archer looked me over. "How in the world did you do it, Lam?" he asked.

I said, "I just kept taunting whoever it was, using the type of approach that would make a man lose his temper or make a frustrated busybody woman open up and give me a piece of her mind."

"You're sure it was a man?"

"I think so."

"What the hell's that, the tape recorder?"

"That," I said, "is a tape recording of the voice. I'm having the calls tape-recorded."

"But what good does it do when no one says anything?"

I said, "We got him talking once. I think we can do it again."

Archer said, "I dropped in just to make sure things were going all right and that your partner would show up. I don't want to leave Miss Chelan unguarded tonight."

"Bertha will be here," I said. "In fact, there she is now," I added, as the bell rang. When Marilyn opened the door, Bertha said, "I suppose you're Marilyn Chelan. I'm Bertha Cool."

Bertha pushed her way into the room, looked at Archer, said, "Hello, what are *you* doing here?"

"Just checking up to make sure you came," Archer said.

Bertha glowered at him. "I said I'd be here. Want me to punch a time clock?"

"I wanted you to be here."

"I'm here."

Archer said, "Now, I don't want to have any misunderstanding about this. I want you to sleep in that twin bed there in the bedroom, Mrs. Cool, and you're to stay with Miss Chelan. You're to keep her in sight every minute of the time until tomorrow morning when Donald Lam comes in.

"Now, Mr. Lam, you'll have had breakfast by the time you arrive in the morning. Miss Chelan and Mrs. Cool will have had breakfast. Then you can take over at nine o'clock in the morning and stay with her all the time tomorrow."

Archer pulled in his stomach and looked very executive.

I turned to Bertha and said, "You know how to work this tape recorder, Bertha. Whenever the phone rings, make a recording of the conversation. If there isn't any conversation, make a recording of the rhythm of the breathing. As soon as the party at the other end of the line hangs up, ring up UL 3-1212 and get a recording of the time."

"Why do you want to do that?" Bertha asked.

"Evidence," I said. "Furthermore, if any more special delivery letters come, don't open them. Save them for evidence. Mark your initials on the envelope and the time of its arrival. But leave the envelope sealed."

"Okay," Bertha said.

Marilyn gave me her hand. "I'll see you tomorrow morning, Donald?"

"Right," I said.

Her smile was trusting and her eyes held mine for three or four long seconds.

I said, "Good night, everybody," and went out.

Chapter 3

I LEFT Marilyn Chelan's apartment, got my car, then looked around on Neddler Drive for a good parking place that would give me a view of the exit of the apartment house.

I found one, backed the agency heap into the curb and waited.

I sat in the car for thirty minutes before Archer came out.

He walked rapidly down the street half a block to where he had his car parked. He was so engrossed in what he had in mind that he was completely oblivious of his surroundings. He never once looked back, but he did look at his wrist watch a couple of times, as though he might have been late for an appointment and was wondering whether the person with whom he had the appointment was going to wait.

He started his car and I tailed along for a block and a half without turning on my lights, taking a chance on getting pinched in order to keep from alarming my quarry.

It was probably a useless precaution, but I took it anyway.

Archer drove to a new little cocktail bar which had opened up to the east of La Brea and north of Hollywood Boulevard, parked his car in the lot reserved for customers of the cocktail bar, went inside and stayed for twenty minutes.

When he came out, he was accompanied by a broad-shouldered man in his early forties, a chap who had kept himself in pretty good condition, all things considered. He was the human dynamo type and while he talked, he made forceful gestures with his hands.

He stood by Archer's car talking with him for a minute or so. Evidently he was doing the talking, because, from time to time, he would push his forefinger into Archer's chest, and Archer, listening attentively, would nod.

Then they shook hands. Archer got in his car and drove off.

I didn't like to pull in too close behind Archer's car for fear this chap would spot me and know that I was tailing Archer. But I didn't want Archer to get away, so after he had a half-block's head start, I stepped on the throttle and came along behind. I took the precaution of looking from one side of the street to the other, as though I was gawking for an address and wasn't the least bit interested in the car ahead.

The man who had been standing in front of the cocktail bar talking with Archer had been getting ready to start his own car. I saw him climbing into an Oldsmobile as I drove by.

Archer started making time. He was going someplace in a hurry. He was a full block ahead of me by the time I got to the corner, and a couple of cars that were going fast cut in between us.

I had the license number of Archer's car and wasn't worried, just so he didn't turn off the street.

He had turned to the left on Franklin and we ran west to La Brea. There was a boulevard stop at La Brea, and I felt the chances that he would go to the right and encounter a dead-end street were negligible, so I didn't pour on the gas again until I had made the boulevard stop, turned to the

28

left and was headed south on La Brea. Then I stepped on it, hogged the traffic and caught up with Archer as he turned to the right on Sunset.

A car that had passed me went on and passed Archer. I fell in behind. We hit a stream of traffic.

Archer pulled into a service station where there was a telephone booth. I lagged behind far enough to pretend to be selecting a parking space at the curb, and saw him get out of the car and enter the telephone booth.

I circled the block.

The guy had just finished dialing on the phone when I swung around the block.

I looked at my watch and made note of the time. It was ten-seven when he hung up.

I moved down a block, turned off my lights, parked the car and waited.

Archer came out, got in his car, drove six blocks to another service station where there was a telephone, got out and entered the phone booth.

I consulted my watch. It was ten-sixteen and twenty seconds when he hung up.

When Archer left that phone booth, he was in a hurry. He drove to Rhoda Avenue and turned left on the avenue.

I brought my car to a stop and watched his taillights.

He went down the street for about three blocks, and then I fell in behind him with my lights out.

All of a sudden I saw the red brake lights on Archer's automobile flare on. The car wavered, then the stop lights went off and the right turning light came on.

I turned on my lights and drove to the right at the first intersection and waited just short of the street which paralleled Rhoda Avenue.

A few seconds later, Archer's car went by, going very fast. He was doubling back.

I had a glimpse of him silhouetted against the lights of the street as he went by. He had his head up, looking in the rearview mirror.

His tires screamed as he turned to the right.

Evidently something had happened to alarm the guy.

I figured he had gone about four blocks altogether down Rhoda Avenue, so I turned back to Rhoda and went on down, looking the situation over. I slowed down and didn't see anything interesting. Then suddenly I saw it!

There was a police car parked in a driveway. A couple of plain-clothes men sat in it, smoking, but their attitude tabbed them for what they were. They were simply sitting there on a stake-out, waiting for some development.

I drove on by and made a right turn, just as Archer had done.

Suddenly headlights came on a block behind me.

I stepped on it, turned to the right, drove a block and turned to the right again.

The car behind me hesitated at the corner, spotted me and turned off its lights.

The officers at first tried to tail me without me knowing anything about it.

I played along, pretending I knew nothing of the police car.

I made a bluff of turning to the left, changed my mind, turned to the right, stepped on the throttle and suddenly made a complete U-turn. I went past the police car, made a quick left turn, drove into a private driveway and turned off all lights and the ignition.

The police car went screaming by.

Lights came on in the house where I had parked. A man in a bathrobe opened the door.

"What do *you* want?" he asked.

I started to get out.

"Bill?" I called confidently.

"Bill who?"

"Addison, of course," I said.

"I don't know any Bill Addison."

"He doesn't live here?" I asked.

"No."

"Well, I'll be damned," I said. "This is the address I have."

I got back in the car, started the motor and backed out of the driveway. I drove half a block and parked. The officers probably had the license number of the car. I was going to need a good story by tomorrow if they wanted to follow up on it. But I didn't dare to take chances on having Archer drive by while the officers were shaking me down, and at the moment there were so many answers I didn't have that I wanted to avoid all questions.

I was where I could watch Rhoda Avenue, about three blocks from the place where Archer had started to turn in to a driveway and then changed his mind.

A big Oldsmobile limped by. The left-hand side had been caved in. A taxicab drove by. There was no sign of the police car driving back to the stake-out.

There was a little traffic, a Ford, a station wagon I took to be a Chevy, another car driving fast. I couldn't get the make.

Then the police car cruised by. The officers either didn't see my car or paid no attention to it.

A car of the same make and model as my agency heap drove by. It was almost crawling. I saw the crippled Oldsmobile again. This time it was going pretty fast.

I looked at my watch.

I'd been there three-quarters of an hour.

I decided the coast should be clear and started the car. I pulled out into the right-hand lane and gave it the gun.

I hadn't gone ten blocks when I met a car that whipped into a U-turn and came up behind me.

A red spotlight flooded the left side of my car and I pulled over to the curb.

The police car pulled up and stopped just behind me. One of the officers got out and came walking over.

"What have I done now?" I asked.

"Let's see your driving license," the officer said.

I gave him the driving license.

"All right, Mr. Lam, how about the registration on the automobile?"

I showed him the registration slip.

"Cool and Lam Detective Agency, eh?" he said.

"That's right."

"What are you doing down here?"

"Oh, I was just driving around," I said.

"Know anybody living on Rhoda Avenue?"

"No."

"How did you happen to turn in to it?"

"Did I?"

"You know you did. Now, can the wisecracks."

"I was shadowing a man down here and lost him, and I thought I could sit tight for a while and then maybe find his car parked somewhere along in here."

"You know his car?"

"It's a Cadillac."

"Give."

I shook my head.

"You heard me," the officer said. "Give. We're not playing games. This is business."

"What kind of business?" I asked.

"Police business."

I said, "There was an accident down the road. The driver of this automobile was a witness. He speeded away. I guess he didn't want to be called as a witness. I felt that I might make something out of it, if I could produce a witness. So I tagged along to see where he went."

"What's the license number?"

"Now, wait a minute," I told him. "You're wanting altogether too much. I can't tell you that. This is the way I make my living."

"Why did you follow him?"

"I wanted to follow him to where he parked, and then I was going to take a look at the registration certificate on the steering post of the automobile, then I was going back and check on the accident, get the numbers of the cars that were involved, find out who was hurt and how bad."

"Ever hear about ambulance chasing?" the officer asked me.

"Sure, I've heard about ambulance chasing," I said. "I haven't solicited anyone yet, and, under the circumstances, I have a perfect right to be a witness."

"To the accident?" the officer asked.

"To the fact that a car that was where the driver could

32

see the accident got in a devil of a hurry getting away from there."

"What's the license number?"

I opened my notebook and gave him one of the license numbers that I keep on tap to alibi myself if I ever get picked up in a situation of this sort.

The officer made a note of the license number. "Okay," he said, "I guess you're clean. But just keep out of this neighborhood."

"Why?"

"Because I told you to, that's all. We don't want a private detective car hanging around here."

"What's the idea?" I asked. "What's going on around here?"

"Nothing," the officer said. "We just don't want you hanging around here, that's all."

I said, "Okay. Some car tried to follow me. It had its lights turned off and I thought maybe my quarry had turned the tables on me and was getting ready to crowd me into the curb and beat me up."

"So what did you do?" the officer asked.

"I used evasive tactics," I said.

"Such as what?"

"I made a sudden turn, then whipped my car in a U-turn and got out of the neighborhood."

"What did you do after that?"

"I shut off the lights and parked, waiting for things to cool down."

The officers looked at each other.

"Now," one of them said, "you're beginning to make sense. We *thought* that you were the car we were tailing a while back, but we couldn't be sure."

"You mean *you* folks were the ones who were tailing me without lights?"

"That's right."

"Well, why the hell," I said, getting indignant, "didn't you turn your red light on and flag me down to the curb if you wanted to know who I was? You scared the hell out of me. I thought I was in for another beating."

33

"You get them often?" the officer asked.

"I'm a private detective," I said, "and I like to work alone."

The officer sized me up speculatively.

"Why didn't you turn your lights on, your red lights?" I repeated. "What was the idea of tailing me with your lights off?"

"You saw us tailing you?"

"Sure I did. I saw you when you turned your lights off."

"You didn't know it was a police car?"

"How the hell was I to know it was a police car?"

"We're asking the questions," the officer said. "You're supposed to give the answers."

I said, "I've lost half an hour of my time, I've lost the deal I was working on, and you've had me scared to death."

"Okay," the officer said, "forget it. Get the hell out of here. And don't hang around this neighborhood."

"Okay," I said, and started the motor.

Suddenly one of the officers said, "Hey, wait a minute."

I shut off the motor.

"There was a car that came down Rhoda Avenue just ahead of you, put on the brakes, started to turn left, then made a right turn. That wasn't the car you were following, was it?"

"I think it was, but I don't know," I said.

"Why don't you know?"

"Because he got away from me. I didn't want to crowd him too close."

"Why not?"

"I didn't want him to know I was on to him."

"You'd followed him this far. Why didn't you get up closer?"

"Because I didn't want to make the guy suspicious. I had got close enough in traffic to get his license number. That was good enough for the time being. Also, I'd had a fair look at him and I thought I could recognize him."

"Which way did he finally go?"

"I don't know. I tell you, I lost him."

34

"All right," the officer said, "get going, and keep out of this territory for a while. We're working on something down here and we don't want some private detective's car flushing our quarry before we're ready. On your way."

I nodded, said, "Don't tell anyone about that license number. That's my ace in the hole."

"Okay," the officer said. "On your way."

I drove on down the street. The police car turned back down toward Rhoda Avenue.

I drove to police headquarters.

I needed an accident which had taken place between 9:40 and 10:15 P.M. I wanted it somewhere in Hollywood. I was willing to give or take a mile or two in any direction, but I couldn't cheat much on the time element. I was also willing to take anything from a hit-and-run to just a fender-brushing, but the time element was important.

In a city the size of greater Los Angeles, there are accidents of varying sorts and degrees and seriousness happening every hour, but a lot of them aren't of sufficient consequence to be reported.

I looked over the traffic reports and found that a man by the name of George Littleton Dix, thirty-six, driving an Olds, had been involved in an accident on North La Brea. There was a dispute whether he had made the boulevard stop at the intersection or had gone right on through. The man who was hit insisted he had gone right on through the boulevard stop. Dix insisted he had brought his car to a full stop. The driver of the car behind Dix was listed as a witness and there was one other witness, a woman. The officer's report didn't mention anything except the bare essentials.

I made notes of the names, the times and the license numbers of the cars involved.

This was to be my life insurance in case the police started checking. And there was, of course, the distinct possibility that they would start checking.

I called it a day, went to my apartment, parked the agency heap in the parking lot and crawled into bed. The time was 1:45 A.M.

I set the alarm for seven o'clock the next morning.

Chapter 4

I SHOWED UP at Marilyn's apartment at five minutes to nine.

She and Bertha had finished breakfast and were washing the dishes in the kitchenette. Marilyn was washing and Bertha was drying.

When Bertha had a chance, she gave me a wink and jerked her head toward the living room.

I went in and sat down.

"Have a good night?" I asked, after I had seated myself.

"Slept like a log," Bertha said from the kitchenette.

"How about you, Marilyn?" I asked cheerfully. "Did you sleep?"

"Not very well. There were two of those phone calls just as we were getting ready for bed."

"What time?"

"A little after ten. Bertha has the times."

Bertha took out a notebook. "They're on the tape recorder," she said. "I checked the time with my watch and with the official time number.

"The first call was completed at seven minutes past ten. The official time, by the time I had dialed and got the number, was seven past ten and twenty seconds. The second call terminated at ten-sixteen and thirty seconds, according to the official time."

"No calls later?"

"No, just those two. We were ready for bed. Marilyn says they kept her from sleeping." Bertha hesitated, then added, "The sonofabitch didn't keep me from sleeping. I slept like a log."

"Any conversation?" I asked.

"Not last night," Bertha said. "Just the heavy breathing."

"You taunted him?" I asked.

36

"I called him everything I could think of, along the lines of his being a yellow-bellied coward."

"Anything else?" I asked.

Abruptly, Bertha said, "You finish up, dearie. I want to talk to my partner."

Bertha dumped the dish towel on the side of the sink, came in and sat down beside the easy chair in which I was seated.

She lowered her voice and said, "Hell's to pay."

"What's the matter?" I asked, keeping my voice low.

"Look at her face," Bertha said. "She's been bawling her eyes out."

"Keep talking," I said. "What happened?"

Bertha said, "We're being framed for fall guys, but I can't prove it, so I decided to play dumb for a while."

"What happened?"

"That damned little minx drugged me."

"How do you know?"

Bertha said, "She made some hot chocolate last night before she went to bed, and hot chocolate is one thing I can't resist. She asked me about what I liked to eat, and I told her I had long since ceased to give a damn about my figure, that I only wanted to keep active and didn't want to get all larded up. I told her I loved a cup of hot chocolate at night, and she said she did, too, and one thing led to another, and she fixed up some hot chocolate for me."

"You think it was drugged?"

"I know damned well it was drugged."

"How?"

"Well," Bertha said, "just before we got into bed, I caught her looking at me a couple of times and there was something calculating about the way she was looking. I had an idea the little minx had something up her sleeve, so I decided I'd pretend to go to sleep and just lie there and listen.

"Well, I lay there pretending to go to sleep, and by God, Donald, I *couldn't* keep my eyes open. I kept fighting a heavy-lidded stupor, and the first thing I knew it was morning and I had the sort of taste in my mouth that comes from a heavy dose of sleeping medicine."

37

"What time did you go to bed?"

"Right after those phone calls. We went to bed early. She said she was all in. We were just drinking the chocolate when the phone calls came in."

"You think she got up and went out last night?" I asked.

"How the hell should I know?" Bertha said. "She did something. My own idea is that this whole bodyguard business is just a blind. My inclination is to give her a damned good going-over."

"Don't do it," I said. "I have some interesting dope. Let's not say anything for the present, let's just ride along with the gag. Don't lose your temper for a while. Is there anything else?"

"I'll give it to you in the order things happened," Bertha said. "There was a special delivery letter at seven o'clock this morning."

"What did you do with it?"

"You left word not to open them."

"That's right."

"We kept it, unopened. It's on the little stand there where she puts mail."

"What was next?" I asked.

"Then the telephone rang about seven-thirty. It was the same old business of breathing hard."

"Did you get the time on the tape recorder?"

"Yes, but I don't know what the hell good that's going to do."

"Never mind that," I said. "What else?"

"Well, about eight o'clock some woman rang up, and Marilyn wouldn't let go of the phone. She said it was a personal message for her. She acted as though she knew the woman and it was just some friendly chat. But while I was standing around, Marilyn was very guarded in what she said. So I made a big business of going to the bathroom and slamming the door. I figured she'd forgotten about the tape recorder. My leaving the room would give her a chance to say anything she was going to say without my hearing it, and then at a later date we could turn on the tape recorder and listen to the conversation."

"Well?" I asked.

"Since that conversation, things have been all shot to hell," Bertha said. "She rang up Jarvis Archer and said she had to see him and she'd like to have him drop in right at nine o'clock."

"Have you listened back on the tape recorder, to find out about the conversation with her and the girl friend?"

"No. There hasn't been any chance so far. I thought that when you came in, you could take over and go through a lot of motions getting caught up on what had happened during the night and getting everything ready for the day. That would give you a good excuse to listen back on the tape recorder. Then we'll see if she makes a kick about you listening in on the personal conversation."

"You're sure the tape recorder was on?"

"Oh, sure," Bertha said. "It's fixed right to the telephone with an induction coil and you can see the light pulsing as the voices make sound. It came in all right. I had the volume adjusted just right, but I didn't have it in the monitoring position so she wouldn't think about the tape recorder."

"Okay," I said, "you follow my lead."

I got up out of the chair, went out to the kitchenette.

"Bertha tells me you telephoned for Mr. Archer," I said.

"Yes."

"What's the trouble, Marilyn?"

"I can't take it any more."

"Did you have any more phone calls?"

"Yes."

"Same as the others?"

"Yes."

"They're on the tape?"

"I guess so. Everything that comes in goes on the tape, doesn't it?"

"Well," I said, "I'll listen and see if I can learn anything. Did Bertha call up for the time?"

"I think she did, yes. The last call was right around seven-thirty."

"You were just having breakfast?"

"No. It was before breakfast. I went back to bed for a while. I didn't sleep at all well."

"Well," I said, "it's all in the day's work, Marilyn. Don't let them get your nanny goat, because that's what they're trying to do. Let's see what his conversation sounds like."

I went back, turned the tape recorder over to rewind, went back a few turns on the spool and turned on the tape.

I heard heavy breathing, then Bertha's voice in a torrent of profane invective, then the sound of the phone hanging up, and after an interval, a voice saying, "The time is ten—oh-seven—and *twenty* seconds . . . The time is ten—oh-seven—and *thirty* seconds . . . The time is ten—oh-seven—and *forty* seconds . . ."

Then there was the sound of the phone being hung up and the tape went on perfectly blank.

I said to Marilyn, "That's one of the calls that came in last night. What happened to the second call last night and the two that came in this morning?"

"I don't know," she said innocently enough. "Aren't they on there?"

I looked at the number on the tape index and said, "What's the use kidding us, Marilyn? You know perfectly well they aren't there. You turned this tape back, listened to the first one of last night's calls, then turned the tape on to the erasing position and erased everything after that."

She met my eyes defiantly. "Well, I have a right to erase my personal telephone conversations. Just because you and Bertha are trying to protect me doesn't give you a license to snoop into my private business."

"You did erase it?"

"Yes, of course I erased it. I didn't want to erase the second call last night, but I had to work fast. I guess I messed things up."

"When did you erase it?"

"While Bertha Cool was flouncing around and going to the bathroom so ostentatiously that she telegraphed what she had in mind, just as effectively as though she'd written it out on a blueprint. She was curious about my personal telephone conversation and she wanted to find out what it was,

40

so she made a big show of going into the bathroom and slamming the door, then running the water, making a lot of racket and giving me a chance to have what I thought would be privacy. Then she intended to come in and play the tape recording of the conversation. Or, rather, have you do it. That's why she went out of the kitchenette when you came in and talked with you in a low voice.

"I wasn't born yesterday and I'm not a child and I don't relish the idea of living the life of a goldfish. When Mr. Archer comes up I'm going to tell him that I can't take it any more. I'm going away. He hired you and he can let you go. I won't need you any more. I'm pulling out."

The buzzer on the apartment door sounded, a long and two shorts, a long and two shorts.

"That will be Mr. Archer now," she said.

She went over and opened the door.

Archer came in all breezily efficient. "Well, well," he said, "we've got the whole gang here this morning—both partners, a session in bank. What seems to be the trouble, Marilyn?"

She said, "I can't take it any more, Mr. Archer."

"Can't take what?"

"All the phone calls, all these special delivery threats, all this business of living like a goldfish in an aquarium, with people staring at every move I make. I'm finished. I'm leaving. Call off your watchdogs."

"Where are you going?"

"You'll never know," she said. "No one will ever know. I'm just going to make sure that no one's following me, and then I'm going to go where no one will *ever* find me. I'm going to stay there for a while until things blow over."

"What things?" I asked.

"How should I know?" she flared at me.

She turned back to Archer and said, "Don't argue with me. My mind is made up. What's more, I'm going to want some money."

"Now, wait a minute," Archer said. "This is coming pretty fast for me, Marilyn. . . . I suggest we sit down and talk it over, and I think you'd better take a little time before you reach a definite decision."

41

"I don't want any time," she said, "and I want to be sure that nobody is going to follow me. I've got everything all fixed up. I've made all my plans. How much money have you got with you in the form of cash?"

Archer hesitated a moment, then extracted a billfold, took out some bills. "I happen to have rather a sizable sum," he said, "about seven hundred and fifty dollars."

"I want three hundred—no, I want four hundred."

"But, Marilyn," he said, "this is—"

"You said you'd see me through this," she interrupted. "Now, I want you to play it my way. We tried it your way and that wasn't so hot. You hired bodyguards and they haven't done a bit of good. Things just keep on the same way. I'm finished."

Archer gravely counted out four one-hundred-dollar bills.

She said, "Now, you sit right here with these detectives. I want to be sure that you keep them here and that no one is following me or trying to follow me."

She calmly walked into the bedroom, opened a closet door, picked up a little suitcase which she had evidently packed surreptitiously without Bertha's knowledge, strode to the door, walked out and said, "Mr. Archer, you're co-operating in this thing and I'm going to thank you to see that I have fifteen minutes before anybody leaves this apartment. Fifteen minutes is all I want. And don't try to do the obvious, like covering the taxicabs or the railway station, or any of the obvious things.

"If *you* could follow me, anybody could follow me. And I'm not going to leave any back trail that *anyone* can follow."

She opened the apartment door.

Bertha Cool said, "Wait a minute, dearie. Let's take this thing in our stride. Let's not go off half-cocked and—"

"Dearie," Marilyn flung at her. "You and your dearie, dearie, dearie! Donald I could take, but you are a pain in the fanny!"

Bertha Cool lurched to her feet. Marilyn slammed the door.

Archer got in her way. "Just a minute, Mrs. Cool. I

42

know Marilyn, and when she gets excited like this, there's not much use—"

Bertha flung him to one side and lunged for the door.

Archer grabbed one of Bertha's arms and hung on. "Just a minute, Mrs. Cool. You're working for me. I order you to let her go."

Bertha jerked her arm loose, sent Archer spinning off balance.

I lit a cigarette.

"You sonofabitch!" Bertha said to Archer.

"Why, Mrs. Cool," Archer said reprovingly, "what language for a lady!"

"Go to hell," Bertha said, starting for the door, jerking it open.

Bertha looked down the corridor, came back and said to me, "Well, *you* were a big help. The elevator was up at this floor, where Archer left it. She's taken it. She'll be long gone by the time I could get that elevator back."

"We're being paid as bodyguards," I said, "not as jailers."

"Now, just a minute," Archer said. "I know you people are upset. I am myself. But I've known Marilyn some time. She's very sensitive, she's very impulsive. When she recovers her self-possession, she's going to feel sorry about this. She'll ring up and apologize. But, in the meantime, I can't say that I blame the poor girl. The strain of having those telephone calls, of receiving those special delivery threatening letters, has been more than she could take.

"Now, it's after nine o'clock and Mr. Lam here came to put in his shift. So we won't quarrel about apportioning the time, and I won't ask for any rebate on the retainer I gave you.

"I'm sorry, Mrs. Cool," he went on. "I hadn't anticipated things would turn out this way. I feel that there has been a mutual misunderstanding. You thought perhaps the job would be slightly different from what it has been, and I had been led to believe that you people could accomplish the impossible.

"Now, we'll just close the books on the entire transaction. I'll take the recorded tape of the telephone calls that I

43

understand you have here, and I believe there were two or three special delivery letters which you didn't open."

"There were two or them we didn't open," Bertha said. "Donald thought there would be fingerprints on them."

"I thought it was difficult, if not impossible, to get fingerprints from paper," Archer said to me.

"It used to be so considered," I told him. "They had to develop the fingerprints with iodine vapors and the results weren't too good. Lately, they've worked out a new process by which the amino acids in the perspiration and natural oil on the fingertips form a chemical combination with the preparations used to glaze the surface of the paper, and latent fingerprints remain for years. They can be developed even years later."

"You're sure about this, Lam?" he asked.

"I'm sure about it."

"Well," he said, "it will be interesting. I know some people who are interested in fingerprints and we'll see what we can do with those special delivery letters."

Archer walked over to the little correspondence table by the door, picked up the special delivery letter.

"Wasn't there one other one?" he asked.

I turned to Bertha. "Was there?"

"There was one that came in yesterday while you were here, wasn't there?"

"That's right," I said, "only it came in later."

"Well," Archer asked, "where is it?"

"I'm sure I can't tell you."

"I'd like to consider the case closed," he said, "and I'll take charge of the evidence."

"Sure," I told him. "Sure. I'll send you anything we have, only we'll keep the tape and the recorder. We only rented them. We have to return them."

He seemed hesitant.

I picked up the tape recorder, swung over to the door, smiled at him, winked at Bertha and said, "Well, that's the way things go. We can't win them all. Okay, let's call it a day. I suppose she'll want us to be sure the apartment is locked. I presume she's taken her key with her so she can come back when she gets good and ready."

"Undoubtedly," Archer said. "She's a very competent young woman. However, if you don't mind, Mr. Lam, let's give her a few minutes more. I like to keep on a basis of strict honesty with my employees. If I tell them I'll do something, I'll do it. She asked that no one leave the apartment for fifteen minutes."

"You didn't promise," I pointed out.

"I gave an implied promise," he said.

Bertha glowered at him for a moment, then sat down.

There was an uncomfortable silence which lasted for nearly a minute, then Bertha said, "This whole damned case looks phony to me."

"It is, of course, an unusual case, I can appreciate that," Archer told her. "And I suppose a person in your business has so many of the usual run of cases that, when one is encountered that doesn't fit into a pattern, it seems to be what you refer to as phony."

"How right you are," Bertha said. "It seems to be what I refer to as phony."

But Bertha made no further effort to follow up on that or to crash the door, and we sat there.

I went over to my easy chair, picked up the morning paper I'd brought in, settled back and read.

Archer studied me curiously for a little while, then finally said, "Well, folks, our fifteen minutes are more than up. I guess we may as well forget the whole business. I'm sorry things turned out the way they did, and I'm very sorry that you weren't able to accomplish more than you did. However, I can appreciate the extreme difficulties under which you were working."

"Extreme difficulties is right," Bertha said. She marched over to the door and jerked it open.

I shook hands with Archer. "I'm very glad I met you," I told him.

He watched me speculatively.

"Let's understand, Lam," he said, "the case, as far as your agency is concerned, has been terminated. I wouldn't want to have any publicity which would embarrass Miss Chelan—the police, for instance."

"I wouldn't want to do *anything* which would embarrass Miss Chelan," I told him. "Shall we leave together, so that if Miss Chelan ever claims that someone ransacked her apartment, we can each give the other an alibi—unless, of course, you should happen to have a key."

"Me have a key to Marilyn's apartment?" Archer exclaimed.

"I was just suggesting the possibility," I said.

"Well, I don't relish the suggestion," he snapped. "Come on, we'll all go out together and *that* will be the end of our business association."

We went out in the corridor. Archer slammed the door.

Bertha ostentatiously doubled back behind his back to try the doorknob and make sure the door was locked.

Chapter 5

ELSIE BRAND, my confidential secretary, said, "Well, I didn't expect to see *you* today. I thought you were baby-sitting."

"We got fired," I said.

"Slapped for speeding?" she asked.

"Pinched for obstructing traffic," I told her. "We weren't moving fast enough."

"You must have been in reverse gear," she said.

"I probably was."

"What sort of young woman was she, Donald? Bertha said she was good-looking."

"Wonderful shape," I said. "Beautiful eyes. Graceful. Long-legged and slim, but beautiful curves, if you know what I mean."

"Donald, stop it. You're just trying to rib me."

46

"But," I told her, "we got paid for the day, because we got a retainer as a guarantee."

"Leave it to Bertha to see to that," she said.

"Leave it to Bertha," I told her. "So now I have a day on my hands that I can devote to the interests of our client."

"You mean the one with the curves?"

"No, I mean the boy friend."

"I thought you said he wasn't a boy friend."

"He said he wasn't a boy friend. I'm not quite that naïve."

"That," she said, "would be the day!"

"How are the crime catalogs getting along?" I asked.

"I'm trying to keep them up-to-date. But I have a shelf overflowing with scrapbooks and the cross-indexing is taking up a lot of time. Bertha's been crabbing about it, but I told her I did it in my spare time."

"Haven't you been doing some at night and on week ends?" I asked.

She averted her eyes, then brought them back to mine. "A little," she admitted.

That had been Elsie's idea of helping me in some of my cases. She'd kept a scrapbook of unsolved cases on which the police were working, so that if at any time we needed information about some case, all she had to do was to go to an assortment of scrapbooks that were elaborately cross-indexed and dig out all the information that had appeared in the newspapers. Three or four times now, we had found the service absolutely invaluable.

I said, "I don't suppose your cross-indexing includes addresses, does it?"

"Why?"

"Out in Hollywood," I said, "there's a Rhoda Avenue. The number I'm interested in is somewhere in the seven-hundred block on Rhoda Avenue, and since it's on that side of the street, it will be an even number."

Elsie shook her head. "Gosh, I'm sorry, Donald, but I haven't kept a cross-index on addresses. I've kept an index of the different types of crime and everything I think will be of value. But the addresses . . . no."

47

She hesitated a moment and then said, "It wouldn't be too much work, however, to make a note of addresses in the future. That is, I could have a big city map and put numbered pins in the different localities and—"

"And then you'd *never* have any week ends or evenings to yourself," I said. "Forget it. You're doing too much as it is."

"Oh, Donald, I do want to help. I know some of the chances you take and the way you play things and how frequently you make some lightning-fast deduction that pays off and—well, things that no one else ever appreciates. . . . And I'd *like* to be of more help."

"You're helping a lot," I told her.

"What about the Rhoda Avenue address—what happened there?"

"Police were staked out on a building there last night," I said, "and I'm afraid I blundered into a situation that may require some explaining."

"What kind of a stake-out?" she asked.

"I don't know," I said. "That's the thing about it that puzzles me. Two cars went by. I was in the second car. The police didn't do anything about the first car."

"Were they watching the cars that went by or watching the house?"

"They were watching the house. That is, I *think* they were. And I don't think they were too much interested in cars that were going by until they saw two go by all at once, so to speak. The first car slowed and swerved as if it was turning in, then the driver changed his mind. My impression was that the cops were staked out on the place for the purpose of watching people who went in, although it's hard to tell."

"What happened?"

"They took after me, missed me for forty or fifty minutes, then I blundered into them and they gave me a shakedown, looked at my driver's license and asked questions."

"What did you tell them?"

"I told them I was checking a witness in an automobile

48

accident that had taken place out in Hollywood. I didn't pin myself down on location and they didn't pin me down."

"Suppose they try pinning you down later on, Donald?"

I grinned and said, "There *was* an accident, one that was made to order, out on North La Brea, and I'm going to get in touch with the people who were involved in the accident and ask enough questions that will register with them. Then, when the police start asking more questions later on today, I can give them some references that will back up my story. In the meantime, you don't know where I am or when I'll be back."

I went on out.

Chapter 6

IT TOOK a little research to get George Littleton Dix located, but I finally found he was sales manager of the firm of Carson, Nelson, Honcutt and Biggs. They were in the real estate business.

A little telephoning elicited the information that they were primarily interested at the moment in a subdivision out in the Van Nuys area and that Dix would be found out there.

I drove out.

The subdivision was a typical Southern California sales promotion, with a portable high-peaked office building, colored flags fluttering in the breeze, signs proclaiming the sun-drenched splendors of the climate, and all the rest of the setup.

The place was well promoted and was attracting a good deal of attention. There were a dozen or so customer cars parked in front of the high-peaked office, and salesmen were escorting potential customers out to various points of vantage, showing them contour maps, pointing out the view possibilities of the different lots.

I went into the office.

A good-looking receptionist was sitting behind a desk marked *Information*.

"Do you have a Mr. Dix here?" I asked. "I have some friends who know him, and—"

"Oh, yes, George Dix," she said. "He's out showing some property right now, but he should be in within a few minutes. In the meantime, would you like to look at some maps, Mr. . . . er . . ."

"Do the maps show the various lots?"

"Oh, yes."

"And they have information about the terms and prices?"

"Yes, there's a complete price list. Was there something in particular that you had in mind, Mr. . . . er . . ."

"The utilities are all in?"

"Oh, yes, indeed. It's a complete, modern subdivision."

I accepted the literature she gave me. "Let me study this for a while," I said.

I went over, sat down and apparently became absorbed in the literature.

Two or three parties came in, had salesmen assigned to them and went out.

Then a rather elderly couple came in, and I heard the girl say, in a low voice, "There's a man waiting for you, Mr. Dix."

I pretended at the moment not to hear but kept my face down over the literature. Then after a moment, when Dix would have had an opportunity to size me up and look the other way, I raised an eye over the literature and then suddenly buried my face in the prospectus again, pulled out a pencil and began doing some figuring.

The two elderly people who stood at the counter and were about to sign the contract were evidently customers who were just buying a lot.

George Dix was the same man I had seen last night talking with Jarvis Archer in front of the cocktail place.

I got up, walked over to the window and stood looking out, apparently checking the view.

Behind me I could feel the tension as Dix wanted to be

sure to close the deal with the couple before turning toward the new customer, but he definitely didn't want *me* to get away.

Fortunately, the elderly couple was cautious. They wanted the answers to lots of questions. They were about to make a check for the down payment and sign the contract, so Dix had to concentrate on answering the questions and staying with them.

I eased out of the place into the open air, stood in front of the door for a moment, carefully keeping my back turned to Dix, then jumped in the agency car and started the motor.

I half expected Dix might run to the door, but he didn't dare leave the people with whom he was just closing.

I got away from there fast and headed back for the office, doing a lot of thinking.

Chapter 7

WHEN I ENTERED the reception room, the door to my private office was open and Elsie Brand was sitting, facing the door. She had moved her chair slightly, so that I could see her as soon as I entered the outer office.

She raised her left hand, the palm out toward me, and held it there for half a second.

I couldn't get the signal, but the fact that she had moved her chair the few inches over to the left and propped the office door open made me realize something was in the wind.

I paused, as though it had suddenly occurred to me that I had forgotten to put a coin in the parking meter, turned back toward the corridor door, planning to go out, then telephone Elsie and find out what the trouble was.

I had made it out of the door and was about halfway to the elevator when I heard the steps behind me. They were hurrying, purposeful, authoritative steps.

"Just a minute, Pint Size."

The voice was that of Sergeant Frank Sellers.

I turned and registered surprise. "Hello, Frank."

"Going someplace?" he asked.

"Just wanted to check something in the car."

"Urgent?"

"Not particularly."

"It can wait?"

"Yes, sure, if there's anything *you* want, it can wait."

"All right, come on in. I want to make talk."

I followed him back into the office.

Sellers said to Elsie Brand, "Do you always keep this door open?"

"No," she said. "It was . . . it was a little close in here."

"What made it close?" Sellers asked.

Before Elsie could answer, I said, "That cigar you're always worrying around with your teeth. Elsie is allergic to the odor of stale tobacco."

"Oh, that," he said, taking the moist cigar stub out of his mouth and looking at it speculatively. "That doesn't smell things up. It isn't even lit."

"You may think it doesn't smell things up," I said. "That's because *your* nose is paralyzed."

"Oh, phooey," he said. "I like to chew on a cigar the way some people like to chew on gum. It doesn't hurt anything. What the hell's the idea of leaving the door open?"

"Airing the place out," I said.

"All right. Come on in and sit down. I know I'm not going to get anything out of you. Why did you expect me?"

"I didn't expect you."

"Okay, Pint Size. You were chasing around down on Rhoda Avenue last night. What the hell was the big idea?"

"I was working."

"What kind of work?"

"What you might call a capital investment."

"In what way?"

"All right," I said, "I'll come clean. I heard an accident out on North La Brea and saw a man driving away rapidly. I thought he was a witness who didn't want to become involved, and, just on general principles, I thought it might be a good idea to find out who the guy was."

"Who was he?"

"I don't know."

"Where was that accident?"

"North La Brea."

"What time?"

"A little after ten o'clock."

"And you followed this escaping witness to Rhoda Avenue?"

"That's right. I was staying pretty far behind."

"Who was he?"

"I don't know."

"What was the license number of his automobile?"

"I can't tell you that."

Sellers looked at me and said, "You wouldn't follow a man all that way without closing in enough to get a good look at him. What did he look like—the driver?"

"I don't know."

"You gave the police a license number last night."

"I know I did. I realize now it was the wrong car."

Sellers said, "It wasn't a mistake. It was a phony."

"What do you mean, a phony?"

Sellers said, "That car is a black Cadillac all right, but, for your information, that car was in Portland, Oregon last night. The driver is on a vacation."

"What the hell!" I exclaimed.

He gimlet-eyed me.

"How come you didn't get the number?"

"I was giving him lots of rope. I may have lost him and tagged after another black Cadillac. He turned in at Rhoda and pretended he was stopping at a house in the middle of a block, then suddenly he changed his mind and went on around the corner. I tried to close the distance then, and I would have got close enough to check the license at that time, but these cops came tagging along behind me in a car with the lights out. I thought I was going to get worked over, so I concentrated on making a getaway."

"All right, give me the real license number of the car you were tailing," Sellers said.

"I tell you, I haven't got it."

"What do you mean, you haven't got it?"

"I was afraid to alarm the guy. I didn't get close enough to get his license number."

"You gave this phony license number to the cops."

"I didn't want to have to explain the whole situation to them."

"You're cutting a hell of a lot of corners," Sellers said, "and I don't believe that you tailed this fellow without getting his license number."

"I tell you, I didn't want to get close enough to scare the guy. He was running away from something."

"That accident?"

"Not the accident. He'd seen it, he didn't want to be a witness, but he was running because of something else."

"Why?"

"I don't know. Maybe he had been calling on some cutie in an apartment house and, just as he was leaving and getting in his car, he saw the accident and was afraid somebody would grab his license number and subpoena him as a witness."

"You talk too glib," Sellers said.

I said, with an aggrieved air, "That's what comes of telling you guys the truth. You just get insulting."

"The trouble with you, Donald," he said, "is that you try to mastermind the game all the time. You try to play your cards part from the top and part from the bottom of the deck, and one never knows where the deal is coming from."

"So," I said, "you play it on the theory that I'm dealing from the bottom of the deck *all* the time?"

"How else would you play it, if you were me?"

"I've never given *you* a bum steer yet," I said.

"The hell you haven't."

"Whenever you've followed my suggestions, you've come out on top of the heap. When you haven't, but have acted on the assumption I've been lying, you haven't done so good."

"Oh, phooey," he said. "Go ahead, rub it in. You've been

54

lucky and you're smart, I'll admit that. But you aren't going to play smart with the police."

"All right, so I'm not playing smart with the police."

"Well, let's find out a little more about this accident," he said.

"I haven't had a chance to look it up in detail yet," I said, "but I got the license numbers of the cars that were involved. There was a big Olds, driven by a fellow with black, wavy hair. He was somewhere around thirty-two or three. The license number was XDA 177. And there was a Ford, the one that was hit. I got the license number of that car."

"All right," Sellers said. "Since you're so smart, who was at fault in the accident? Did the guy in the Olds make the boulevard stop or didn't he?"

I said, "I would prefer not to answer that question at this time."

"Oh, is that so, Pint Size? Well, I'd prefer to have you answer it at this time—right now."

"All right," I said. "I'll tell you frankly, I don't know."

"You don't know? You saw the accident, didn't you?"

"No. I heard the crash and came along right after the accident. Then I saw this car that suddenly pulled out and speeded up. From the way the guy was driving, I had a hunch he'd seen the accident and was trying to get away. So I sensed an opportunity to do a little good for the partnership by checking on him. I tried to follow him so he wouldn't be suspicious.

"Well, people had begun to stop on account of the crash and I had a little trouble getting through the congestion. This car was a couple of blocks ahead of me. I got delayed at a traffic signal, but I'm pretty well satisfied I picked up the same car on Sunset. It looked like the same car."

"And you couldn't get the license number?"

"No. I didn't try at that time. I wanted to find out where this fellow was going in such a hurry. In order to do that, I didn't want to sneak up on him and alarm him. So I kept in the background and coasted along behind him, just making sure I could keep him in sight but laying far enough behind so that he wouldn't get suspicious. If I'd speeded up and got the license number, that's all I'd have had. I decided to play it smart by tagging him to wherever he was going. Then I'd close in for the license number *after* he'd reached the place he was headed for in such a hurry."

"That's the part of it that sounds fishy to me," Sellers said. I kept quiet.

"You wouldn't lie to me, would you?" Sellers asked.

"Look," I told him, "you've pushed me around enough so I'd lie to you any time I had to, to protect a client. There's one thing I'll tell you straight from the shoulder— Any time I come to you and tell you that I think you should do a certain thing or that it would be to your advantage to play the thing a certain way, I'm on the level."

"I know. That's the trouble," he said. "You want to do my thinking for me."

"I'm not trying to think for you. I'm simply telling you that any time I make a suggestion to you, I'm on the up and up."

"This damned caper of yours sounds fishy as hell to me," he said. "Now, I'm going to tell you something else—I want you to forget it."

"What do you mean, forget it?"

"Exactly what I said. You're lying, but we're willing to forget it if you are. Don't go messing around with this thing any further. Don't get into it any deeper. Don't try to sell what you know to the parties involved in the accident. Don't try to pick up a client out of that automobile accident business. Don't talk to newspaper reporters."

"Good heavens," I said, putting all the synthetic surprise I could into my voice. "You mean to say, just a little old two-bit automobile accident like this is going to attract the attention of reporters and—"

"That isn't what I said," Sellers said. He extended his index finger and pushed it into my chest, with little jabbing motions emphasizing his words. "I told you to forget it. I told you not to tell anybody about this. I told you not to get mixed up in that automobile accident. In other words, I'm telling you to keep your nose clean on this, or you'll get hurt so bad you never will get over it.

"And now I'll take my soggy cigar and my obnoxious presence out of your office, and if you try to cut any corners on this, I'll personally see that you're finished as a private detective. You never will get a license renewal."

Sellers stalked out of the office.

"What the hell," I said to Elsie Brand. "Now, what do you suppose brought that on?"

"While he was waiting for you to come in," she said, "he was nervous as a cat. He was pacing back and forth and rolling that soggy cigar around in his mouth."

"Did he ask to see Bertha when he came in?"

"No, he wanted to see you. I felt he didn't want to see Bertha, didn't want her to know he was in the office."

"He and Bertha get along," I said. "I don't get along with him because he . . . well, because he feels I'm trying to mastermind the cases where our paths cross."

Her smile was demure. She started to say something, then checked herself and went on with her typing. After a moment, she said casually, "And, of course, you *wouldn't* do anything like that, Donald."

"Of course not," I said. "I'm going out, just in case Bertha should start asking questions. I'll be back after lunch."

Chapter 8

ELSIE BRAND was coming out of Bertha's office as I entered the reception office and did a diagonal over to the door of my private office.

Elsie timed herself so we met at the door.

"Bertha looking for me?" I asked.

She shook her head. "She wants me to file time sheets on how much office time I'm putting in on your crime files."

"What did you tell her?"

"Told her I would."

"I'll have a little talk with Bertha," I said. "In the meantime, make me an estimate of the amount of such work you've done on your own time in the last month. . . . And forget this time sheet business."

"I found out about the Rhoda Avenue mystery," she said, closing the door.

"How come?" I asked.

"It was on the radio. I tuned in the news just in case, and when I saw what it was, I made shorthand notes. Do you want to listen?"

"Give me a condensation first. What was it?"

"A murder," she said.

"Where?"

"762 Rhoda Avenue."

"Oh-oh," I said. "This could be serious. Who was killed?"

She said, "A Jeanette Latty was murdered sometime last night in a bungalow at 762 Rhoda Avenue."

"Any clues, motive, or anything?" I asked.

She said, "Apparently Jeanette Latty was running an escort service sort of a thing, furnishing attractive girls for dates."

"You mean call girls?"

"No, the— Well, at least—Donald, you embarrass me. It's hard to describe the difference."

"I could describe it in a few words," I said. "I will, if I have to. Now, go ahead and tell me. You're a big girl now, you know."

"Well, they weren't actually . . . well, they weren't call girls, but the police had been asked to check on her activities."

"How come?"

"A radio reporter, who doesn't get along with the police department and who has been riding them on a lot of vice stuff, claims the police had been asked to check and that this woman had been running an unlicensed escort service."

"What sort of a service?"

"According to a statement that Jeanette Latty had made a week or two earlier, the girls were all nice, refined girls who were banded together on a co-operative basis to pick up some money on the side by accepting dates. It wasn't a

58

regular escort service. They didn't advertise. It was just a private affair. The understanding was that there would be no passes, that the girls were simply partners for men who were strangers in town. The clients were respectable out-of-town executives with the highest references, who wanted to go around and see the town and didn't want to do it alone. Mrs. Latty would arrange an interview, find out the type of man she was dealing with, and if he met the requirements, would call for one of the girls to come down and meet him. She'd perform introductions and she'd establish the rules very firmly in the customer's mind.

"The men never knew where the girls lived. They thought the Latty house was their residence. They would call for them at the bungalow, go out for the evening, bring the girls back to the bungalow and say good night to them there. They thought the girls' mother lived there.

"The whole thing was on a high-class, co-operative basis, with all the profits above a basic hourly rate going into a pool.

"There was no escort agency within the meaning of the law. It was simply a co-operative deal by unattached young women to get an evening's entertainment, dinner, dancing and a fee. In turn, they furnished entertainment and high-class companionship to some out-of-town executives and high-class businessmen.

"At least, that was the way Mrs. Latty told the story."

"What were the rates?" I asked.

"A minimum fee and an hourly charge. They didn't stress it on the radio, but the girls who went out were pretty much on their own. They were supposed to be girls who knew how to take care of themselves, and— Well, I suppose if they wanted to violate the rules that Mrs. Latty had laid down, and if the customer wanted to violate the rules, there was nothing to stop them."

Elsie blushed.

"Good heavens," I said in mock amazement, "do you suppose anything like that actually happened?"

"Donald, don't."

"What about the murder?"

"Someone used a round rock in a woman's woolen stocking, knocked her out, then strangled her with a silk stocking. Police found her body about nine o'clock this morning. They have the murder weapon. Evidently she'd been killed last night, probably sometime between ten o'clock last night and three o'clock this morning."

"Strangled?" I asked.

"That was the cause of death, but she had been hit on the head with this impromptu blackjack. Someone slugged her, knocked her unconscious and then finished the job with the stocking."

"That," I said, "explains a lot."

"How come?"

I said, "Police were sitting on the house. They had a stake-out. What they wanted was to get the license numbers of the automobiles that drove up. They were getting a list of the people who were in on the play."

"How do you know, Donald?"

"Because I was there," I said, "and because I probably furnished the break that pulled the police away from the job at just about the time the murder was being committed."

"That's what Frank Sellers wanted to find out?" she asked.

I said, "He wanted me to keep quiet about what I knew."

"Why?"

I said, "Figure what a spot the police would be in. They're having a feud with this radio reporter. He'd like to get something on them.

"Now, here's the situation. Jeanette Latty was running an escort service. She claimed it was a co-operative amateur deal, where the girls went out with hand-picked, selected clients and didn't do anything improper. As long as that's the situation, the police had their hands tied. But if they could find the girls doing anything immoral, the situation would be different. Or, if Jeanette Latty advertised or held herself out as running a professional escort service, the situation was different."

"So what?" Elsie asked. "I don't get it."

"So," I said, "the police decided to move in on the job sometime last night and put a stake-out on the house. They knew they'd have a hell of a time trying to shadow the girls when they went out on dates, catch them doing something immoral and then proving that Jeanette Latty knew what was going on.

"So they decided to tackle it from the other end. John Doe, a big tycoon visiting from out of town, would hear about this delightful amateur escort service where he could get a girl who wasn't a professional but was still willing to go out and show him the town, and the rest would be up to him as a salesman."

"Go on," she said.

"John Doe is vulnerable. He can't hold out on the police. The idea of having his name tangled up in a vice investigation would scare him to death.

"So the police simply sit there waiting. A car drives up. John Doe brings his date home, says a very formal good night and drives back to town. It may be a rented car, a private car, or a taxicab. Police get the numbers on the license.

"The police have no difficulty tracing the guy. They find he's John Doe, a big shot from out of town who is registered at one of the hotels. They drop in to see him. John Doe is frightened silly.

"They say, 'Look here, Mr. Doe, we'll keep your name out of this, provided you co-operate with the police. If you don't co-operate with the police, you're in it up to your necktie. We're investigating an escort service run by Jeanette Latty out on Rhoda Avenue. You patronized that escort service. We want to know how you heard about it. We want to know all about the girl you were out with. We want to know what happened, and when it happened and where it happened, and whether you gave the girl money, and, if so, for what.' "

"I see," she said.

"So," I said, "they had a stake-out on the house."

"Well, what's wrong with that? Isn't that what the police would be expected to do?"

"Sure," I said. "But they weren't trying to seal the place up. They were just getting information, getting license numbers, and getting material to work with."

"And when you followed this other car, they thought there was something fishy?"

"The other car started to turn in. They let it go. Then I came, following the other car, and all of a sudden they decided there was something there they should investigate, so they took after me and I ditched them, and that made them even more suspicious. So they cruised around until they finally spotted me. They had an idea I had holed up somewhere in the neighborhood."

"And then they shook you down?" she asked.

"They shook me down," I said, "and I had the right answers. A private detective was about the only thing that would have fitted into the picture. They felt that I was shadowing somebody trying to get evidence on him in a divorce action. They didn't believe my story about the automobile accident, they didn't want to tip their hands, so they chased me out of the neighborhood and then went back to their stake-out on the house at Rhoda Avenue."

"But why should they be so anxious to have you forget about this, Donald?"

"Because," I said, with a grin, "you can figure where it puts the police. They were watching the house and the murder was committed right under their eyes, probably during the time they had been decoyed away on a wild-goose chase. That doesn't make the police look very efficient."

"No," she said thoughtfully. "That could be played up by a smart and hostile radio reporter who was gunning for the police department, so it would look very bad indeed."

"Therefore," I said, "Frank Sellers, who knows me personally, comes down to throw a scare into me and tell me to forget it."

"And you're going to forget it?" she asked.

"Hell," I said, "I can't forget it. The guy who was going down there intending to turn in to the Rhoda Avenue house was our client in this baby-sitting case."

"But he got scared away?"

"He saw the police car parked there, and he's smart. He wasn't like some fellow bringing home his date for the evening. He was alone in the car; he saw a police car parked

62

there and he shied off. Then, while the police were thinking that over, I came along, evidently tailing him, and the cops decided they'd take a look."

"And where does that leave you?" she asked.

"Right in the middle," I said. "The police want me to forget it and I can't forget it."

"Why not?"

"Because," I said, "our ex-client, Jarvis C. Archer, could damned well have ditched me, and while I was playing tag with the police, could have gone back to the house and murdered Jeanette Latty."

Elsie looked at me with big, startled eyes and said, "But the police don't want you—"

"The police want me to forget it," I said.

"Suppose you don't forget it?"

"Then," I said, "it's not entirely inconceivable that the police could claim that during the forty-five minutes I was holed up in the neighborhood I had detoured back to the house on Rhoda Avenue and strangled Jeanette Latty. Stranger things have happened."

"You're going to keep working on it?" she asked.

"I'm going to try and get a little more knowledge," I said. "Knowledge is power. And, in a deal of this sort, a lot depends on what you can find out."

"Where do you begin?" she asked.

"I begin with you," I told her.

"With me?"

"Yes."

"What do I know?"

"Nothing yet," I said, "but you're going to find out something. Ring up the office of the Molybdenum Steel Research Importing Company and ask for the personnel manager."

"Then what?"

"Tell him, or her, that you want to apply for a job as secretary."

"What name do I give?"

"You won't have to give any," I said. "Just tell them that you would like to make an appointment to discuss a position as secretary. They'll tell you that you should first visit a certain employment agency, that that agency has charge of all their placements."

Elsie looked at me for a moment, then picked up the telephone book, found the number, dialed it and asked to be connected with the personnel department.

She was quite convincing over the telephone. "I am a thoroughly trained private secretary," she said. "I would. like to have an appointment for the purpose of discussing my qualifications and the possibility of employment with your company."

I heard the squawking noises which came over the receiver, then Elsie took her pen and hurriedly wrote, "Pacific Screening & Personnel Agency, Ladd Building."

Elsie said, "Thank you," and hung up.

She gave me a quickly questioning glance, then, at my nod, looked up the Pacific Screening & Personnel Agency, got them on the phone.

"This is Donald Lam," I said, "of the firm of Cool and Lam. We're a private detective agency and I'm trying to get a credit reference on an employee who was placed in a job through your agency."

"I'm afraid we can't help you, Mr. Lam. We get everything we can about qualifications and references, but we don't go into matters of credit," a cool, feminine voice on the other end of the line assured me.

"I understand," I said, "but if I could get a line on the references, I can take it from there. You will understand, of course, that helping establish the credit of an employee is very much to the benefit of the employee."

"I understand," she said.

"With whom should I talk?" I asked.

"Probably with Mr. Frank Eckelson."

"Thank you," I said. "I'll try and see him. Is he in the office now, do you know?"

"He was a few minutes ago. I think he'll be in this afternoon."

"Thank you," I said, and hung up.

Elsie Brand regarded me with apprehensive eyes. "Donald,

you keep fooling around with this thing and you'll be in danger."

"I know it," I told her. "And if I don't keep fooling around with it, I'll be in danger. Once some radio reporter starts putting the heat on the police department, the police are going to look for a fall guy."

"Donald, I wish you wouldn't."

I grinned at her. "I wish I didn't have to," I said, and went out.

Chapter 9

FRANK ECKELSON was about forty-two or forty-three. He used half glasses for reading and, for other work, peered over the top of his glasses. He had watery blue eyes, bushy eyebrows and a high, wrinkled forehead. The wrinkles came from continually looking up over the top of his reading glasses.

"I'm trying to establish credit on a secretary you placed," I said. "Marilyn Chelan. You got her a job with the Molybdenum Steel Research Importing Company. If you can give me just a little something on her background, I'll take it from there."

"Why did you want to know, Mr. Lam?"

"Credit."

"We don't inquire into credit."

"I know," I told him. "I do. That's my business."

"A private detective?" he asked.

"We do this work in our spare time," I said. "With an office overhead these days, you have to keep busy. And this business is either feast or famine. We're either working so hard we're burning the candle at both ends, or else trying to find something to fill in."

I yawned with elaborate indifference in order to show him that this was just another routine chore.

The yawn reassured him. He went over to a filing case and said, "She came here from out of town."

"I know," I told him. "Salt Lake City. I've got a line out there, but I'd like to check personally. What were her local references?"

"She didn't have any local references— Wait a minute. . . . She was staying with a friend, a Pauline Garson, in the Vector Apartments, and she gave Miss Garson as a reference."

"You followed that up?" I asked.

"Frankly," he said, "we did not. She gave the names of her last employers and we checked with them and we saw letters from them. Then I turned her over to our secretarial manager for a series of tests as to typing, shorthand and general I.Q."

"You give all applicants tests?"

"Certainly," he said. "We're not just an employment agency with a lot of lists. We do screening and personnel work. When one of our clients asks for an employee with certain qualifications, we try to give him one whose qualifications are *exactly* what is required."

"Thank you," I said. "I'll check with Salt Lake City."

I left his office in the Ladd Building and drove out to the Vector Apartments. The directory showed a Pauline Garson in Apartment 211.

I went back to the office, opened the door of the outer office, nodded to the receptionist, walked on toward my private office and gave only a casual glance to the man whose face was buried in a copy of the *Wall Street Journal* and who was waiting in the reception room.

Elsie Brand said, "Did you see the man waiting outside?"

"For me?" I asked.

She nodded.

"Who is it?" I asked.

"His name," she said, "is George Littleton Dix— Why, what's the matter, Donald?"

66

I said, "Now, how the hell do you suppose he got wise to me?"

"Why, Donald? Who is he?"

I said, "He's someone I wanted to avoid. That is, I didn't want him to know I was interested in him."

"But you are interested in him?"

"I am and I was, and somehow he's found it out."

The phone rang.

Elsie answered it and said, "The receptionist wants to know if you can see Mr. Dix now."

"Tell him to come in," I said. "Let's find out what the guy has in mind and get it over with."

"What is it, Donald? What's the trouble?"

"The minute he finds out that I was working on that babysitting case, the fat's in the fire," I said. "He probably doesn't know it yet, but he will."

"And then?" she asked.

"Then," I said, "I'm caught with my hand in the cooky jar. Go on out and bring him in, Elsie."

Elsie escorted Dix into my office.

"How do you do, how do you do," Dix said, with the brisk synthetic cordiality of a supersalesman.

"Mr. Lam, I don't want you to think that I'm being unduly persistent. I am, in fact, solving something of a mystery."

He kept gripping my hand and pumping it up and down.

I decided to beat him to the punch, grinned at him and said, "Well, while you're solving mysteries, you can tell me how it happened *you* sought *me* out, because I was looking for you earlier in the day."

"So I understand," he said.

"You do?" I exclaimed, letting my voice and face show surprise.

He nodded.

I said, "I was interested in getting some property out in some of the new residential subdivisions that are being opened and I guess you've made something of a name for yourself as a saleman, because one of my clients told me that George Littleton Dix had taken care of her in connection with the purchase of a lot and that she had found everything was exactly as represented, that you were scrupulously honest and had really made a supreme effort to see that she got exactly the lot she wanted."

"Well, what do you know," Dix said. "Who was she?"

I said, "Her name was— Now, wait a minute . . . I guess I shouldn't have said that."

"Why not?"

I said, "I let you know first that she was a client of ours. We don't give out the names of our clients. That's entirely confidential. If I had just told you I had talked with a customer of yours, there wouldn't have been any difficulty whatever. But I went a little farther than that and told you that she had been a client of ours, or was a client of ours, and that ties my hands."

"I see your point," he said, beaming. "I can understand the situation. Well, I'll be very glad to tell you about our subdivision out there and to do something for you in the selection of a choice lot. You understand, Mr. Lam, all lots are not equally desirable. They seem to be equally desirable to the people who lay out the plats, and the prices are the same, but to us veteran real estate operators who have been in the game for some time and have gone through a good many subdivisions and had the benefit of experience, and, if I may say so, the benefit of hindsight, we can see quite a difference.

"Naturally, I try to protect my clients. I pick out the lots that I think are the most desirable and sell them to the people I'm taking care of personally—probably it was that, that your client referred to."

"I'm quite sure it was," I said.

"You were out to see me earlier today?"

"Yes, I was. I was working on a very thin time margin, however, and couldn't have done very much except get acquainted with you and get a prospectus, and then have an opportunity to take the matter up with my partner."

"Oh, this is a partnership investment?"

"It may be," I said.

"Well, I have a prospectus with me, and if you'll just take

a look at this map, I can show you a couple of *very* desirable lots that are left. If, however, you're buying this for a partnership investment, you might want to have a block of lots."

He looked up hopefully.

I shook my head. "No," I said, "it's not that big an investment. I was thinking of getting a building site for a house, and I thought perhaps my partner, Bertha Cool, would like to build in the same neighborhood. I was going to take it up with her."

"I see," he said.

"But," I pointed out, "this doesn't cover *your* business with *me*. It certainly is a remarkable coincidence that you happened to come in here."

"No coincidence at all," he said, "just good, plain business."

"I'm afraid I don't understand."

"I could," he said, "hand you the usual line of hooey that I had been having a late lunch in the neighborhood and just dropped in because I knew you'd been out there earlier in the day and hadn't waited."

"How did you know that, if it's a fair question?"

He laughed and said, "It's a fair question. We're in business, you know, Lam, and I'm a hustler. I don't mind telling you that my commissions are just about as much as all of the rest of the salesmen on the project put together.

"I have my own system of operation. I give out a lot of cards to various prospects and they come in and ask for me. If I'm busy and any prospect doesn't wait but gets up and moves out, the girl at the desk has very definite instructions. She goes to the ladies' rest room. We have a spotting telescope mounted in there, right by the window. She gets the license number of the automobile in which the person is driving away, and I look up the registration. Then I make it a point to drop in and see that person. I'm particularly interested in finding out what happened and why he didn't wait, whether something had happened to offend him or whether, as in your case, it was the press of other business."

"You're going to a lot of trouble," I said.

"No, I'm not. There are very, very few people who walk out on me. But once they do, I make it a point to find out why. I can't afford to have some of my potential customers disgruntled or offended over something. I just wanted to make sure that you weren't offended."

"I'm not," I said. "I was just busy."

"I'm going to leave you a prospectus, Mr. Lam, and I'd like to make an appointment with you. Could I see you and your partner tomorrow afternoon? You just fix the time and I'll arrange to be there."

"I'm sorry, but I can't do that, because my partner is very busy right now and she's just informed me that there's a new case coming in that I'm going to have to work on. It will be several days before I am free again, but if you'll leave me a prospectus I'll get out your way within a week or so."

"Oh, that's too bad," he said, "because I'm afraid some of these choice lots will be gone."

"That's a chance I have to take," I told him.

He said, "I'll tell you what I'll do, Lam. There's one lot that I know is going to be available. A person made a deposit on it and the check bounced. Now, we haven't officially terminated the contract yet, and I'll hold that for four or five days. You can get out there within that time and take a look at this lot. It's a really choice lot, much better than the average. If you find that you like it, then we'll go in and terminate the contract because of the bum check and make out a new contract in your name. How's that?"

"That will be fine," I said, "only don't hold anything open, because my time is going to be pretty well taken up during the next few days and I may not be able to get out."

"That's all right. That's quite all right, Lam. We're glad to do it for you. . . . Now then, there's another matter . . ."

His voice trailed off into silence.

"Yes?" I asked.

"There's just a chance," he said, "that you scratch my back and I'll scratch yours."

"Meaning what?"

"Well, I am involved in a little altercation where I may need some private detectives, some good ones."

"What's the trouble?"

"I had a little accident, and the other party claimed I didn't make a boulevard stop and that I had been drinking. That's all bosh and nonsense."

"Did you have a breath test?" I asked.

"No, I didn't, not at the time. But I got to thinking things over, and a couple of hours later I dropped in at the police station and asked to have a breath test."

"They made it?"

"Yes. They found a trace, only a small trace of alcohol, something like seven per cent, I believe it was."

"Of course, that is not necessarily an indication of what it had been a couple of hours before."

"Well, I know, but it shows I wasn't drunk, the way the other person claimed. Now, I made that boulevard stop, all right. I think the insurance company is going to make a prompt settlement, just because of the nuisance value. But in case the settlement shouldn't go through, I want to get some witnesses who will swear that I made the boulevard stop."

"Did you get the names of any of the people who were there at the time?"

"Unfortunately, I didn't. I got into an argument with the man who was driving this other car, and I guess the witnesses just sort of got away."

"And he didn't get any?"

"Oh, but he did—that's the point. He got a couple of people who really don't know a damned thing about it, who swore that I didn't make the boulevard stop. That's where the trouble comes in."

"How much damage?"

"Very little, very little—to his car. The left side of my Olds was pretty well stove in. I'll pay for that myself. I'm forced to drive a rented car in the meantime. It's a confounded nuisance."

"Well," I said, "we'd have to discuss the matter when the time came for you to hire a detective agency. We're very

71

busy right now and I'd want you to meet my partner, Mrs. Cool. You could let us know if the settlement doesn't go through."

"That'll be fine, Lam. Nobody's made any definite commitments, we're just talking now."

"That's the same way about the lot," I said. "Remember, no definite commitments."

"No definite commitments," he said, and shook hands.

I stood in the doorway and watched him across the outer office, through the exit door and to the elevator.

"Do you suppose he came all the way up here just because you drove away from a subdivision?" Elsie asked.

"I don't know," I told her. "And that's what bothers me."

Chapter 10

I WENT OUT to the Vector Apartments and found a parking place, then I went to a phone booth and phoned Pauline Garson's apartment. There was no answer.

I waited half an hour and phoned again.

A throaty feminine voice said, "Hello."

I spoke with all the assurance in the world. "Pauline?"

"Why, yes," she said.

I said, "Put Marilyn on the phone—quick. It's important."

"Why— Who are you?"

"Nix on it, nix on it," I said. "Seconds are precious. Put Marilyn on the phone."

"Just a minute," she said.

She left the phone and I could hear low-voiced conversation. Then, after a moment, Marilyn's voice on the phone, very timid and diffident, said, "Yes . . . hello."

I started breathing heavily in the phone.

There was a scream at the other end of the line and the phone was hung up.

I went back to the agency car and waited.

Fifteen minutes later a taxicab drew up in front of the apartment house. A cabdriver got out, looked at the directory and rang Pauline Garson's apartment.

I crossed over to the cabdriver.

"Know what this is?" I asked him.

He looked at me, then at my hand and grinned. "It looks like a twenty-dollar bill," he said.

"That's right," I told him. "I'm the one that ordered the cab. Here's twenty dollars. When I raise my hat, take off fast and go back to your cabstand."

"No other place?"

"No other place, just back to your cabstand."

He looked at me with a puzzled expression and I said, "Get going if you want this twenty. Get in your cab and start the motor running, and when I put my hand to my hat, start off."

"Just put your hand to your hat?" he asked.

"Oh," I said, "I'll try to find some excuse. If there happens to be a babe around, I'll speak to her and she'll give me the icy stare. But you watch my hand. When it goes to my hat, take off."

"Okay," he said, got in the cab and started the motor.

About thirty seconds later, a white-faced Marilyn Chelan came out carrying a little suitcase.

I raised my hand to my hat, removed it, said, "Hello, Marilyn. You're coming with me."

"You!" she exclaimed.

"That's right," I told her.

The cab took off from the curb.

"Hey!" Marilyn tried to call after him, but the cab was gone.

I said, "Things have taken a turn that I don't like, Marilyn, and I'm—"

"But I told you, I didn't want you any more. Mr. Archer told you, you were fired. I have no money to hire a private detective."

I said, "You stand here in the doorway and you're playing right into their hands. Now, do you want to come with

73

me and have me take you to a place where no one can find you?"

"Could you do that, Donald?"

"What do you suppose I'm here for?"

She looked at me and said, "I don't know."

I took her arm in one hand, the little suitcase in the other, said, "Come on, Marilyn. The first thing to do is to get out of here before they know you're leaving."

I piloted her over to the agency car.

"How did you know where I . . . where to find me?" she asked.

"It's a cinch," I said. "And if I found you, the other people could find you."

"They found me already."

I stopped dead in my tracks and looked at her in dismay. "They have?"

"Yes. Just within the last half hour. The phone rang and somebody told my friend that they had to talk with me."

"And what happened?"

"The same thing, the same breathing, then silence."

"Just that one call?" I asked.

She said, "The phone was ringing four or five times during the afternoon, but I wouldn't answer it. I promised Pauline that I wouldn't go out and that I wouldn't answer the phone. I never want to see another telephone as long as I live."

I said, "This thing is a lot deeper and a lot more sinister than I thought. Now, I've got to take care of you."

"But why? Mr. Archer told you—I don't have any money for detectives. I'm going to use the money I have to go a long way from here."

"I know," I told her. "I don't want money. I'm going to play it on a contingency basis."

"What do you mean by that?"

I said, "When I find the people who are back of this thing, I'm going to put the bite on them."

"The bite?"

"That's right. I'm going to make them donate."

"How?"

74

"You leave that to me," I said. "They've been pushing you around and it's time for you to quit being a punching bag. It's about time for you to start hitting back."

"Donald," she said, "I wish I knew I could trust you. I feel that I can, and yet . . . there's something about you. You're just too darned cool and collected and . . . you seem to be just a little too sure of yourself."

"That's just my professional manner," I told her. "I cultivate that in order to reassure clients."

"Well, it doesn't reassure me—somehow, it doesn't ring true. You should be a little . . ."

"Frightened?" I asked.

"Not exactly frightened, but more groping in the dark. You seem to know exactly where you're going."

"I do," I told her, opening the door of the agency car. "Get in."

I tossed her suitcase in the back seat, and Marilyn climbed in the right-hand side of the front seat. I walked around and got in at the driver's side and started the car.

"Where are we going?" she asked.

"First," I said, "we're going someplace where nobody can find you. You're not going to hear any more of those telephone calls."

"I wish I could believe you on that."

"All right," I said, "that's a good test. You think I'm cocksure. If you have any more of those telephone calls, you'll know that I'm just four-flushing."

"If you could give me relief from those, if I could have a decent night's sleep without having to take sleeping pills, it would be just absolutely wonderful. As it is, every time I go to sleep I have those horrible nightmares, and then I wake up in a cold sweat, just waiting for that phone to ring."

"Forget it," I told her. "You're among friends."

"I wish I could feel that. I feel so alone and helpless."

"How did you happen to go to Pauline Garson's place?" I asked.

"It was the only place I had to go."

"You've known her for a while?"

75

"It was through her that I left my job in Salt Lake City. She had a line on this job that I am now holding. It seems that Pauline is friendly with the personnel manager of the Pacific Screening and Personnel Agency, and they handle all of the employment for the company where I am working. She learned that there was a good—a real good—secretarial job open, and she knew my qualifications and knew that I could take all the tests and breeze through."

"So you gave up your job in Salt Lake and came here on the strength of—"

"No, no," she said. "I had a vacation coming, so I took my two weeks' vacation, took a plane, came on here and Pauline introduced me to her friend . . ."

"I know," I said. "Frank Eckelson."

"No, not Mr. Eckelson. I had to clear with him, but her friend was Donna Hendrix, who does all the personnel testing for secretaries.

"Mr. Eckelson checked my background and references, then turned me over to Donna Hendrix, and she put me through my paces, with dictation, typing, composing letters, speed, accuracy and all that."

"And you passed?"

"Oh, sure," she said. "I'm really competent. . . . Donald, where are we going?"

"We're just driving around for a while," I said, "to make absolutely certain that we're not being followed. I'm looking for a signal that is just changing and— Here we are."

The signal ahead had turned to amber and I gunned the car through just as it turned red.

"Look back," I said, "and see if anyone is following."

"No, you're the last one through," she said. "Everybody else stopped. You really ran a red light that time, Donald."

"I was in the intersection while the light was amber," I told her.

"I know, but it changed when you were halfway through."

"That's what I wanted. Hang on," I said.

I put the car into a turn, we ran down a side street, then made a left turn and I started gunning the car. "Go on,"

I said, "tell me some more about how you got to Pauline Garson's."

"I had phoned Pauline earlier this morning and asked her to be in front of my apartment house at nine o'clock this morning and wait until I came out. I didn't dare to try to take a taxicab, because I felt sure they'd trace me. . . . Donald, who in the world do you suppose they are? Who is going to all this trouble to harass me, and what in the world is it they want?"

"I don't know," I told her. "That's what we have to find out. After we get the answers to what we want and who they are, we'll take steps to counterattack."

"I wish," she said viciously, "you could just arrange to have that man, whoever he is, given a damned good beating."

"Now, wait a minute," I said, "don't talk like that. It might be held against you sometime. Just take it easy. You let me do the worrying and the fighting. You just sit easy."

"Where are we going, Donald?"

"Where would you like to go?"

"I don't know. I've got to go someplace where I can't—I just can't be left alone, that's all."

"Would you like to hide in Bertha Cool's apartment?"

"Heavens, no. She irritates me to death. She's too . . . too dominating."

I said, "I have a secretary who has an apartment by herself. I think she'd let you stay there."

"That would be rather a strain, living with a stranger."

"Any other friends?" I asked.

"No."

"None at all?"

"None."

I said, "We're going to my secretary's apartment for a while anyway. You two can size each other up."

"But you're not getting paid for all this," she protested.

"I'm going to get paid. And remember this, Archer gave us a retainer. I'm still working on that retainer."

"Donald, you're playing some kind of game."

"I'm playing a game," I told her. "The object of that

game is to find out who's pushing you around and put the shoe on the other foot and start pushing them."

"And why?"

I said, "I hate to be outwitted. I hate to have somebody pull a fast one on me. Now, we didn't do so good on your case. We went in there as bodyguards to try and protect you, and the telephone calls kept on, the special delivery threats continued to arrive, and you got so frightened you became almost hysterical and had to leave. I don't like that."

"You still haven't told me how you found me at Pauline's."

"I'm a detective," I said. "I'd have found you wherever you were."

"But you couldn't have."

"But I did, didn't I?"

"That's the part I can't understand."

I said, "Come on, we're going up to my secretary's apartment where we can talk and where I can look you in the eyes without having to concentrate on my driving."

"But isn't that one of the places where they'd look for me?"

"That's the last place," I said.

"Why?"

"For various reasons. The people who are in this thing think that our connection with the case has been terminated. They can't understand a detective agency having . . . well, what I might call a pride of performance. They think that Cool and Lam are all washed up, as far as the case is concerned. They *might* trace you as far as Pauline Garson's, and then they'd lose the trail."

"I . . . I wish you'd tell me how in the world you traced me."

I said, "Let's put it this way. What did you intend to do when you left Pauline's? You'd called a taxicab. Don't you know it's easy to trace a taxicab?"

"Sure it is," she said, "but I was going to go to the airport, I was going to mingle around with crowds, I was going to get another taxicab, I was going to go to the Union Depot, I was going to mingle around with crowds there. I was

78

going to get another taxi, I was going to make sure I wasn't followed, and then . . ."

"And then?" I asked.

"Then," she said, "I just didn't know. I was going to cross that bridge when I came to it."

"Going to try to leave town?"

She said, "I have some friends in Salt Lake City. Some of them are rather powerful politically. I think they'd protect me."

"And you intended to get to Salt Lake City?"

"Yes."

"From the airport?"

"No. I was going to rent a car from a drive-yourself agency, drive to Las Vegas and then take a plane from there and turn the car in there."

I said, "You can't rent a car without showing them your driving license. That's one of the first things people would look for. They'd try to find your back trail by covering the car rental agencies."

"I never thought of that," she said.

"There are lots of things you haven't thought of," I told her. "Now, sit back and relax, because I want to concentrate on driving and make sure that no one is following us."

I made a lot of elaborate block circlings and figure eights in order to convince her that I was trying to throw off any pursuit, and then drove to a place in front of Elsie Brand's apartment house, parked the car and shut off the motor.

"How long do I stay here?" she asked.

"Until you tell me the truth," I told her.

"The truth?"

"But I've told you the truth."

"No, you haven't."

"Donald, I have. I swear that I have."

I said, "You didn't tell me about Pauline Garson's call this morning."

She looked at me and started to say something, then her jaws sagged and she was speechless for a few moments.

"Go on," I said, "tell me about it. And how many other

people around here have your quote unlisted number end quote?"

She started to say something, changed her mind, then said, "N-nobody. But how did you know about that?"

"I knew about it."

"But I . . . I erased that tape in the tape recorder. . . . Donald, was my phone tapped?"

"Certainly not," I said. "You can't tap a phone on a deal of that sort."

"Then how did you know?"

I said, "Let's put it this way. I used my powers of deduction. You told me you had asked Pauline to have her car parked in front of the apartment house at nine o'clock and to wait for you to come out. You didn't call Pauline, because Bertha was there. Therefore, Pauline must have called you. That was the conversation Bertha heard, the one you erased from the tape, the call you had when Bertha went into the bathroom."

She looked at me with wide eyes.

"Where did you go last night after you gave Bertha Cool the drugged chocolate?" I asked.

She looked at me with wide, panic-stricken eyes. "Donald, whatever in the world are you talking about?"

"Go on," I said. "You're just sparring for time."

"How did you know I went anywhere?"

"It sticks out all over you."

"Donald, can I trust you?"

"What do you mean?"

"Can I count on you to keep anything I tell you in absolute confidence?"

I said, "You can count on me to do whatever is for your best interests, as long as I'm not sticking my own neck out. And that's just as far as you can go. You're my client. Archer hired us to protect you, not him. I'm loyal to *your* interests—as far as I can go. You'd better trust me. It will be better that way."

"Have you read the afternoon papers, Donald?"

"What does that have to do with it?" I asked.

"There's something in there about . . . about a woman

80

who was murdered, a woman they think was acting as sort of a madam, a procurer of call girls."

"Jeanette Latty?" I asked.

"Yes. You know, then?"

"I know," I said. "What's your connection with her?"

"I . . . I went out on a couple of dates."

"That she arranged?"

"Yes."

"What kind of dates?"

"These were on the up-and-up, Donald. I got fifty dollars and taxi fare, but I think . . . well, I think I didn't do what was expected of me, because after that, Mrs. Latty never had any dates for me."

"What do you think was expected of you?"

"Do I have to draw you a diagram?"

"One of those dates was with Archer?"

"Good heavens, no! Archer doesn't know anything about it. He doesn't have the least idea. If he did, he'd . . . he'd drop me like a hot potato. He'd wash his hands of me in a minute."

I did some quick thinking.

"You came here from Salt Lake City?"

"Yes."

"You had some friends here?"

"Only one."

"Who?"

"Pauline Garson."

"And how did you happen to get in touch with Jeanette Latty?"

"Through a girl I'd known in Salt Lake City who— Well, I wrote her how lonely I was, and she told me to look up Jeanette Latty."

"And you did?"

"Yes."

"And gave references?"

"Oh, she talked with me, asked me a lot of questions about whether I had a husband in the background and about boy friends and things of that sort."

"And then got you a couple of dates?"

"Yes."

"Both with the same man?"

"No, heavens, no."

"What do you mean by that?"

"Well, the first man—I would never have gone out with *him* again."

"And the second man?"

"He was better, but— Well, he laughed at me and called me old-fashioned. I don't think *he'd* ever go out with *me* again."

"So," I said, taking a shot in the dark, "last night you had to have a showdown with Jeanette Latty. Why?"

"Because— Oh, Donald."

"Go ahead," I said. "Let's have it all."

She said, "It suddenly occurred to me, because of something that happened, that Jeanette Latty might have been back of all those telephone calls."

"What caused you to think that?"

"Because I got to thinking about the way the envelopes were addressed—the rubber stamp. And I remembered that I'd seen one of those little portable printing outfits out at Mrs. Latty's the first night I went out here. She had been setting some type with tweezers. . . . You know the sort of thing I mean. You get them at the toy stores. They have a holder that will hold three or four lines of type and then a font of rubber type and some tweezers and ink pad, and you can set the type and then put it on the pad and get a pretty good inked impression."

"So what?"

"I got to thinking of that yesterday afternoon late, and I started to tell you about it. Then I thought that I'd better not, because I was afraid if you went out and talked with Mrs. Latty and she should tell you anything about me and the fact that I'd been out on some of those dates . . . well, if Mr. Archer should ever hear of that, why, it would be good-by job and good-by everything."

"So what did you do?" I asked.

She said, "I made up my mind I'd go see Mrs. Latty myself."

"And you did?"

"Yes."

"You drugged Bertha's chocolate?"

"I don't like to use the word drugged. I— Well, I thought Mrs. Cool looked tired and I wanted to be sure she had a good night's sleep, and I had some sleeping capsules that I knew were harmless and— All right, Donald, I dissolved two of those in Mrs. Cool's chocolate."

"Then waited for her to go to sleep?"

"Yes."

"Then took your car?"

"My car was so I couldn't get at it. I called a cab after I got downstairs."

"You got in the cab and went out to Mrs. Latty's?"

"Yes."

"What time was it?"

"Heavens, I don't know, around— It was after Mrs. Cool got to sleep and got to snoring. . . . Oh, I guess it was around ten-thirty, eleven, somewhere in there—I didn't pay any attention to the time."

"All right. You went out and talked with Mrs. Latty and then how did you get back? Did you have the cab wait, or—"

"No, no, I didn't talk with her."

"You didn't?"

"No."

"Why not?"

"Well, the front of the house was dark when I got there, but there was a light in back and I started around to the back of the house, and then I saw the light was on in a bedroom and I could hear Mrs. Latty talking with someone, talking very rapidly and very earnestly, and I thought perhaps I'd better wait for a while. . . . But I sort of hesitated, wondering who was in the room with her, and then I heard a man's voice."

"Did you hear the words?"

"No, just the rumble of a man's voice. But I knew it was a man from the deep tones."

"Were they arguing?"

"I don't know whether it was an argument or not, but—

83

Well, she was talking a blue streak and seemed to be trying to explain something or trying to get the man to do something, and . . . well— You see, Mrs. Latty never wanted to have a lot of cars parked in front of her place. She said she had nosy neighbors and too much activity around the place would arouse curiosity. . . . So I asked the cabdriver to go down in the next block and wait.

"Well, I waited around for a while for this man to go and he didn't go. I could tell from the way Mrs. Latty was talking that she was all worked up about something, and the thought of facing her while she was in that mood was disquieting. I guess I'm just a coward on a deal of that sort.

"Anyhow, standing there I made up my mind I'd go to South America or somewhere, to get away from everything. That's when I decided to try to get Mr. Archer to give me getaway money."

"So you went back to the cab and rode home?"

"Donald, the cab was gone. I guess he got tired of waiting. Anyhow, he wasn't there where I'd told him to wait. I had to walk ten blocks to a bus line. I came home on a late bus."

I said, "You left a back trail a mile wide."

"What do you mean?"

I said, "The cabdriver will read the paper and remember the address. He'll tell the police."

She looked at me with white-faced dismay. "Donald!" she exclaimed. "He wouldn't do that. He's a *nice* guy."

"What the heck did you think?" I said. "That the police are that dumb? Don't be silly. What I'm trying to reconstruct is the time element."

"Why?"

"It doesn't need to concern you at the present time, but I want to find out exactly when you went out there. I'll have to do some checking.

"As far as the police are concerned, you're going to be hotter than a firecracker. You don't dare to use an assumed name, because that would be evidence of flight, and evidence of flight in this state is evidence of guilt."

"Guilty of what?" she asked. "I didn't do anything wrong.

84

I guess that was the trouble, that's why Mrs. Latty didn't want me any more."

I said, "Guilty of murder."

"Of murder!" she exclaimed.

I nodded.

"Donald, they couldn't."

"They could and they will," I said. "Now then, tell me, when did the first of these telephone calls come in? When was the first message you received telling you to get out?"

She said, "I'll never forget the day. It was the fifth. I received a special delivery letter and it had one of those printed threats in it, and then within fifteen minutes I got the first telephone call."

"What time?"

"It was in the afternoon. I had just returned from work. I'd had a shower and was cooking something for supper. I hadn't put on my dress, because I wanted to do the dishes and didn't want to take a chance on getting something on the dress."

"That was on the fifth?"

"Yes."

"And on the fourth you'd been out on a date?"

"You mean one of the Jeanette Latty dates?"

"Yes."

"Heavens, no. I hadn't been out on a date from her place for ten days or two weeks. I just had those two dates, Donald."

"How far apart?"

"Let's see . . . the first one was on a Wednesday and the next one was on the following Friday."

"Mrs. Latty gave you instructions as to what you were to do?"

"Oh, yes, there were printed instructions, printed rules. And I was warned that if I violated those rules, I would be in hot water and would never get any more dates."

"And you didn't violate them?"

"No, I lived up to them scrupulously."

"All right," I said. "The mysterious calls started on the

fifth. Now, let's think back a bit. What did you do on the fourth?"

"The fourth? Why, that was just routine."

"What about the third?"

She knitted her brows. "I can't turn my memory on and off like that, Donald, but I think . . . I'm quite sure the third was routine, too."

"What's routine?" I asked.

"Why, breakfast of grapefruit, coffee, toast—after a shower, of course—then up to the office and the coffee break, then an hour at lunch."

"What do you eat at lunch?"

"I eat a pretty good lunch, but I work crossword puzzles while I'm eating. I'm a nut on them."

"Then you worked crossword puzzles at lunch?"

"Yes."

"On the third?"

"Yes."

"And the fourth?"

"Yes, I think I must have, although I can't remember clearly now."

"What about the evenings?"

"On one of those nights I went to a movie. I treated myself to a cocktail, a dinner and then a movie."

"You went alone to the cocktail and dinner?"

"That's right. They didn't want to let me into the cocktail bar alone. I had a little trouble at first, but I'd been there once before and the waiter knew me. I told him I was waiting for my escort to join me, that I was a little early."

"That was not true?"

"That was not true. I fibbed in order to get in, but I didn't want to sit down at the dinner table and have a cocktail thrown at me by the cocktail waitress, with another special check and a double tip."

"See anybody you knew at the cocktail bar?"

"I . . ." She stopped abruptly.

"Yes?" I asked.

"Yes. I saw some girls I'd seen before."

"Friends?"

"People I'd seen—they worked through Mrs. Latty. I think they were her girls."

At that moment, Elsie Brand turned in the side street and started looking for a parking place.

I opened the car door.

"Come on," I said to Marilyn. "Here's Elsie. I want you to meet her."

Chapter 11

ELSIE BRAND didn't see us until I tapped on the horn, then she recognized me and her face lit up.

She pulled off to the side.

I helped Marilyn out of the car.

"What is it, Donald?" Elsie asked, looking curiously at Marilyn.

"Something I want you to do for me."

"Okay. Anything," she said.

I performed the introductions.

"Marilyn Chelan," Elsie said thoughtfully. "Haven't I heard your name or seen your name on the office records? I'm Donald Lam's personal secretary, you know."

"We were doing a bodyguard job on Miss Chelan," I said.

"Oh," Elsie said.

"I want to talk with her. I want a witness present, and I'm going to have to explore her mind to find out something she knows that she doesn't know she knows. You're going to have to help me."

"Right now?" she asked. "Before we eat? Of course, I can whip up something if you're not too ravenously hungry, but I haven't any meat in the place. I was going to have bacon and scrambled eggs."

"We'll talk first and eat afterwards," I said. "We'll go out to dinner."

"No, no," Marilyn said. "I just want to get where no one can see me. I want to get away from those horrible phone calls and—"

I knew Elsie loved good food, so I said, "Okay, we'll talk a little while and then I'll go out and buy some good thick tenderloin steaks. We'll cook them in the broiler, and in the meantime, Elsie can put some potatoes in the oven to bake. When they're done, we'll take them out, split them open, put in some butter and cheese and put them back in the oven. I'll get a big can of onion rings, some French bread and a bottle of red wine. How does that sound?"

"That," Elsie said, "sounds wonderful."

"I don't think I'll have much appetite," Marilyn said, "but it sounds— Well, those are appetizing words."

We moved on up to Elsie's apartment.

Elsie said, "You'll pardon me while I get the grime and stains of an afternoon at the office removed, and then I'll join you."

Marilyn looked at me. "Where am I going to stay tonight, Donald?"

"We'll cross that bridge when we come to it," I told her.

"What did you mean by saying that you wanted to find out something I knew that I didn't know I knew?"

"Exactly that," I said. "I think something happened on the fourth that you have forgotten about that was significant."

Her eyes suddenly faltered before my direct gaze.

"Remember what it was now?" I asked.

"No," she said.

I said, "Settle down and make yourself comfortable."

Elsie emerged from the bathroom looking fresh as a daisy and studied Marilyn Chelan the way one girl studies another— a visual inventory that took in everything from the head to the feet and all points in between.

I said, "To begin with, I want both of you to understand that our firm was retained to protect Marilyn here from things that had been annoying her. Marilyn became impatient when she didn't think we were getting the results we should and got

Jarvis Archer, who had been footing the bill, to send us on our way.

"Somehow, I think Marilyn is running away from something, although she probably doesn't know what it is she's running away from. That is, she has only a vague idea. I think, however, that Marilyn knows a little more about the way Jeanette Latty transacted her business than she is telling us."

"No, no," Marilyn said. "I've told you everything, Donald."

"Rules were given you?" I asked.

"Yes."

"Printed rules?"

"Yes."

"You wouldn't have kept a copy, would you?"

"I think I have one."

She opened her purse and started fumbling.

It was the usual assortment of stuff found in a woman's purse.

She took out a little folder and extracted two pieces of paper from the folder. One of them was a partially filled-out crossword puzzle, the other was a paper with printing on it.

She unfolded the printed paper and handed it to me.

The rules were a first-class whitewash job. Any time there was a police investigation, Jeanette Latty had fixed things so she could pull out those rules and have herself covered with whitewash.

The printed rules read:

This is a co-operative escort service. You are one of a corps of young women who have banded together to derive amusement, compensation and pleasant company from an evening's work.

You will make no attempt to pry into the personal life of the person who is escorting you.

You will, under no circumstances, permit any familiarities which would not be consistent with women of the highest character.

89

You will not accept any tips or gratuities or any money.

The gentleman who has asked for your company has paid a fee of fifty dollars to the co-operative fund. Twenty per cent of that fifty dollars is withheld to cover executive costs and business overhead. The remaining forty goes to you.

Under no circumstances will you permit the gentleman to escort you to the place where you live, give him your telephone number or any personal information. You will tell him you are living here with me. You will return to the offices of the Bonded Social Service at 762 Rhoda Avenue on the termination of your date. Tell him your mother lives here and you live with her.

The gentleman will then go his way, and only after that will you be free to take a cab to your home.

The cost of the cab both ways is a part of the expense the gentleman is called upon to pay, over and above the fifty dollars which is paid for your companionship. He doesn't know it is cab fare. The escort service pays off the cab.

The gentleman will, of course, pay all costs of entertainment in connection with the evening. And it is permissible to accept from him, in silver, tips for powder room attendants, and he may, if he wishes, furnish you with a corsage or with money for flowers.

You must bear in mind that any violation of these rules may result in causing great embarrassment to the Bonded Social Service and to the other young women who are a part of the organization.

You are required to be in by no later than 1:30 A.M., and you will use every effort to see that the gentleman with you has you at the Rhoda Avenue address by that time.

Personal intimacies are limited to no more than one or two good-night kisses. Parking in automobiles, necking, or engaging in periods of personal privacy are against the rules. It is understood, when the gentleman takes you out, that he wants a companion for a night club, a theater, dancing and similar amusements. You are to be aware of this at all times and to gently but firmly rebuke any attempt at pawings, passionate necking or similar familiarities.

"You adhered to these rules?" I asked.

"To the letter," she said.

"And you think the gentlemen were disappointed?"

"I *think*," she said, "that one of the men had used Jeanette Latty's service before and I think that he thought those rules were made to be violated."

"Which one?" I asked. "The man who took you out the first time, or the one who took you out the second time?"

"Well . . . both, the second one, in particular."

"What's this?" I asked, picking up the crossword puzzle.

She said, "I have an hour at noon. I don't like to hurry through lunch and then go back to the office, and I don't like to go out and walk the sidewalks. I have a cafeteria near the office, I get a table which is uncrowded and clip the crossword puzzle from the morning paper. I don't try too hard to solve it, just enough to give me something to do while I'm eating. I nibble at food and work on the crossword puzzle. Then, at ten minutes to one, I leave.

"Sometimes I have the puzzle finished, sometimes I don't."

"Why did you save this one?" I asked.

"Because," she said, "there were a couple of words in it I just couldn't get and I wanted to see the answer the next day. You know the way the papers do. They publish a crossword puzzle one day and the answer to the crossword puzzle of the preceding day."

"All right, what day was this?" I asked.

She puckered her forehead and said. "That was— Let's see . . . that was the fifth."

"Then why didn't you get the answer on the sixth and throw this away?"

"Something happened to the newspaper on the sixth. I was terribly annoyed. I get the newspaper which comes to the office, and— Well, someone had taken out the part that had the crossword puzzle, the sporting section and a few things like that."

"And you didn't care enough about the crossword puzzle to buy another paper after you quit work that evening?"

"That's right. I went to a movie that night."

"That was the night you bought yourself a drink and a dinner?"

"No, that was the night before. That night was the fourth. I had a drink and a dinner and sort of watched people dancing and just soaked up a little of the bright lights. I didn't stay very late, because I had fibbed about my escort coming in, and when he didn't show up, the headwaiter raised his eyebrows rather significantly when I said I guessed my escort had been delayed and I'd go ahead and order dinner on my own."

"Then on the fifth these telephone calls started?" I asked.

"That's right," she said. "I . . ."

The door chimes sounded.

I frowned and said, "If it's all right with you, Elsie, I think Marilyn had better step into the bathroom and freshen herself up a bit. I don't want anyone to know she's here."

"Do you want her to stay here with me, Donald?" she asked.

"I don't know yet," I said.

I nodded to Marilyn.

She slipped into the bathroom just as the door chimes sounded again, then there were peremptory knuckles on the panel. Bertha Cool's voice called, "Come on, open up. I'm in a hurry."

Elsie gave me a frightened glance.

I went over and opened the door.

92

An indignant Bertha Cool came barging into the room.

"I've been trying to get you all afternoon," she said. "It's a wonder you wouldn't phone into the office once in a while and let people know where you could be located. This may be important."

I said, "Sit down, Bertha."

Bertha glowered at Elsie, then turned to me and said, "It's getting so that whenever I want to locate you, I have to get hold of Elsie. I just had an idea you might be here, so I drove by and, sure enough, there was Elsie's car down there at the curb and your car snuggled right up beside it as though it might be the mating season for automobiles."

Bertha glowered.

"What's on your mind, Bertha?" I asked.

"That little minx who tried to make a stooge out of me," Bertha said.

"What about her?"

"Just a minute and I'll tell you what about her!"

Bertha stalked over to the telephone, picked it up, dialed a number, said, "Dispatcher?"

After a moment, she said, "This is Bertha Cool. You get hold of Sergeant Sellers on the intercom and tell him I've located Donald Lam at Elsie Brand's apartment. I'm up there now."

Bertha gave the address and hung up.

She came back and heaved herself down in a chair and said, "Nobody's going to take this agency for a run-around, not while I have anything to do with it."

"What do you mean, a run-around, Bertha?"

"You know damned good and well what I mean. That whole case was phony."

"In what way?"

"All those phone calls and that heavy breathing, and all that kind of crap. The whole thing was an inside job, all fixed up to give that little twerp an alibi for the evening.

"Whenever she's questioned about where she was, she'll say, 'Why, I was home in bed.' And someone asks, 'Have you got any proof of that?' and she says, 'I certainly have, I had been subjected to a lot of annoyance from anonymous

93

telephone calls and special delivery letters, and I had retained a firm of detectives to act as bodyguards and Mrs. Bertha Cool of the firm of Cool and Lam was right in the room with me all night. I couldn't have left without wakening her.' "

And then Bertha went on, her eyes glittering, "She'll probably go on and add a lot of extraneous details about the fact that she lay there and listened to me snoring, or something of that sort."

"I think you're unduly suspicious, Bertha," I said.

"All right," Bertha said, "keep thinking I'm unduly suspicious. I'm a detective. When I start after something I try to get the answers. When some twerp takes me for a ride, I try to find out why."

"Got any answers in this case?" I asked.

"You're damned right," Bertha said.

"What are they?"

"I told you that chocolate was drugged. You just laughed about it, but when I got up this morning, those chocolate cups were on the side of the sink. I knew my cup because it had a little nick out of the rim near the handle. There was some chocolate left in there. I took a piece of blotter paper, soaked up the chocolate and had a test run.

"They couldn't tell about the quantity, but the test showed very definitely there was barbiturate in the chocolate."

"That still doesn't prove anything," I said. "Maybe Marilyn just wanted to be sure and sleep, and wanted you to——"

"Oh, shut up," Bertha said. "Whenever there's a woman in the case, she flashes a lot of nylon at you, works her eyes back and forth and up and down, flutters a sigh or two, wriggles her fanny, comes through with a tear and then gives you a passionate kiss and you're not worth a damn from that time on!"

"All right," I said, "go on, Bertha. What else did you do?"

Bertha said, "I just called up the cab company and asked them if they had sent a cab to the Neddler Arms Apartments last night between ten o'clock and midnight. My God, the way that little twerp was so anxious to get me in bed and dead to the world, I should have been suspicious right at the start."

"What about the taxicab company?" I asked.

"Nothing to it," Bertha said. "She ordered a cab by phone. The cabdriver came around there about ten-thirty, and Marilyn was there waiting for him."

"And how does Frank Sellers enter into this?" I asked.

"Frank Sellers enters into it," Bertha said, "because that little twerp had the cabdriver take her to 762 Rhoda Avenue, and, in case you don't know it, Jeanette Latty, a procurer or procuress, or whatever the hell you call it, was murdered at that address and the police fix the time of the murder at sometime between ten o'clock and three in the morning.

"Now then, Donald Lam, start making excuses for her on *that* kind of a setup."

I started to say something, but the chimes sounded again, then Sellers' voice saying, "Open up."

Bertha opened the door for him.

"Got anything?" Sellers asked.

"You're damned right I've got something," Bertha said. "That trollop ordered a cab, which got there about ten-thirty and took her out to 762 Rhoda Avenue.

"I drove out to find what was so all-fired attractive out there and found that this madam had been murdered last night. *That's* when I called you."

"Good work, Bertha," Sellers said, and glowered at me. "How's Donald mixed in all this?"

"I don't know yet," Bertha said. "Let's find out. Unless I miss my guess, Donald's been fooling around with the babe. He thought she was on the up-and-up. Why, that frame-up smelled to heaven. The whole thing was a frame-up, from start to finish. Those telephone calls, the special delivery letters, all that sobbing and whimpering—the whole damned thing! It was just a frame-up so she could have an alibi for herself that night."

"That makes it premeditated, first-degree murder," Sellers said.

"You telling me?" Bertha asked.

I said, "You're going a long ways on the strength of one

taxi ride. Is the driver sure he can remember her well enough to identify her?"

"He damned well better be, if he wants to keep driving a cab in this city," Sellers said grimly. "Now then, how the hell are we going to pick up this gal, Bertha?"

Bertha looked at me and shrugged.

Sellers looked at me. "That Latty murder," he said, "is hot. We're in bad on it because we were staked out on the place. We didn't expect anything to happen until along about one or two o'clock in the morning, when the escorts would begin to drive the girls back. We wanted to shadow one or two of the men and shake them down for a statement."

"Why the men?" I asked.

"Because the girls would lie like hell in order to protect themselves," Sellers said. "The men would, at the start, but once we threatened to expose them to the press in the event they *didn't* co-operate, but offered to keep their names out of circulation if they told us the whole story, those guys would cave in. We've done it before. It's an old story with us."

"Well," Bertha said, "you can— What the hell's that?"

"What?" Sellers asked.

Bertha pointed to the two handbags. "One of them is Elsie's," she said. "Who the hell owns the other one?"

Sellers made a swoop for Marilyn's bag.

"Well, I'll be go to hell," Bertha said, glaring at me angrily. "You've already been softened up and now you're running true to form."

Bertha heaved herself up out of the chair, walked over to the bathroom door, tried the knob, then rattled it and said, "All right, Marilyn, get the hell out of there—you've got company."

Nothing happened for a minute.

Bertha said, "You want me to smash this door down and drag you out?"

There was a sound of a bolt and Marilyn opened the door.

"This the one?" Sellers asked.

"That's the one," Bertha said.

"Okay," Sellers said. "We'll get the cabdriver to make an

96

identification. Come on, sister, you're going to take a little ride."

Sellers turned to Bertha. "Usually we can handle things without the help of amateurs, but this time you've given us a big lift, Bertha. We're not going to forget it."

Sellers turned and looked searchingly at me. "And we're not going to forget *your* part in this, either, Pint Size."

"You mean *I* did you a good turn?" I asked.

Sellers drew his extended forefinger across his throat in a cutting gesture.

"Oh yes," he said, "you were giving us your usual co-operation."

I said, "If you hadn't beat the gun, I could have done a lot more for you than that."

"Yes, I know, I know," Sellers said. He turned to Marilyn. "Come on, sister, this is the police."

"You got a warrant?" I asked.

"You know god-damned well we haven't got a warrant," Sellers said. "We're taking her in for questioning. We're going to confront her with the taxi driver."

I said, "Phooey! You haven't got anything in the world against her except the statement of a taxi driver that he took some woman from the Neddler Arms Apartments to 762 Rhoda Avenue on the night a murder was committed. Picking up a fare that way wouldn't mean a damned thing. Even if he makes an identification, some smart lawyer would rip him up and back and down the front."

"Says you," Sellers said.

"Watch him," Bertha said. "He isn't talking to you, Sellers. He's trying to coach the girl. She's got her hooks in him already. My God, what women do to that guy!"

Marilyn was standing white-faced and trembling.

Sellers said, "Now, don't take it like that, sister. We're as anxious as you are to get this thing cleaned up. We want to get the guilty party. If you're the guilty party, that's one thing. If you've committed a murder, we're against you. If you haven't committed a murder, we're for you. You tell us the story, tell us the whole truth, put your cards on the table, and we'll give you the benefit of an impartial investigation."

Marilyn looked at me. I shook my head.

"Come on," Sellers said.

"Do I have to go, Donald?" she asked.

"You're damned right you have to go," Sellers said. "You're tied into this case deep enough so we've got to have you answer some questions, look into your past a little bit, and let that taxi driver look you over and see if you're the woman who ordered a cab to drive you out to Jeanette Latty's place."

I said, "The murderer would hardly call up a cab company, take a cab out to commit a murder, then drive back to her address, leaving such a broad trail for the police."

"How do you know what a murderer would do?" Sellers asked. "I've been in this business all my life and they do some of the damnedest things you ever saw. Come on, sister, let's go."

Bertha looked from me to Elsie. "I suppose," she said meaningly, *"you'd* like to stay here."

Sellers led the girl out. Bertha Cool went barging along in the rear.

The door swung shut.

"Donald," Elsie said, "do you suppose she *could* have committed that crime?"

"At this stage of the game, I don't know," I said. "But there are a lot of things I want to find out. How am I going to get a paper of the sixth, that has the answer to this crossword puzzle that was published on the fifth?"

"Right here," she said. "I fold and save my old newspapers and then pool them with those of the other girls in adjoining apartments and sell them as scrap paper. That's better than having to pay for having them carted away."

"I want the part with the crossword puzzle, the sporting section and— Let's see, that will have the financial section and the obituaries."

"And what do we look for?"

I thought for a moment and said, "Pictures."

"Pictures?" she asked.

98

"That's right," I said, "pictures. Somebody didn't want Marilyn to see something that was in that paper. The news item probably doesn't mean anything, because sporting or financial news wouldn't enter into it. But the girl has a photographic memory for names and faces, and I wouldn't be too surprised if there wasn't a picture in there that might mean something to her."

"And the picture?" Elsie asked.

"I'll make a guess," I said, "a blind stab in the dark. I'll bet the picture is that of George Littleton Dix, with an announcement that he has just been promoted to sales manager of his big new subdivision, with a lot of hooey about him."

"And if Marilyn had seen that picture?"

"Then Marilyn would have recognized him as a man with whom she had been out on a date fixed up by Jeanette Latty."

"All right," Elsie said, "let's get the paper and see. If you say that's what it will be, Donald, I'm willing to bet that's what it will be."

She got the paper. There was nothing in it about Dix.

The crossword puzzle department was in the section containing the sporting news, the stock market report and financial news, the weather and the obituaries.

According to Marilyn, that had been all that was missing from the paper, that one section.

I spread the section out on the table in Elsie's apartment and went through it again and again, looking at pictures.

A sports commentator had his picture at the head of his column. That picture ran daily. The same was true of a commentator on financial trends. There were some action pictures of a player caught stealing second and being tagged out, a picture of a player making a one-handed catch against the left field fence. But none of those pictures was sufficiently clear to be significant.

There were several small pictures in the obituary column and one large picture, the picture of Baxter C. Gillett, the noted financier who had started on a vacation trip with his wife, only to suffer a heart attack in a Santa Monica motel. His wife was with him at the time he died.

There was a good half page describing the activities and financial holdings of Baxter Gillett, who was president of a bank in Santa Ana and head of numerous interlocking enterprises.

I folded the paper over for a last time, then paused and thought for a moment, then turned back to the picture of Gillett.

"Something?" Elsie Brand asked.

"Hang it, it has to be this picture. It's the only one in the whole section that's big enough to mean a thing."

"But, Donald, what possible connection could there be between a Santa Ana financier and Marilyn Chelan?"

"Probably none, when you look at it that way," I said. "But when you look at it from the standpoint of the missing section of the paper and the lack of any other picture— There's something strange here, at that. Let's look at it from another angle.

"The guy was leaving on a vacation. He and his wife were planning on taking a trip up through the Pacific Northwest."

"What's wrong with that?" she asked.

I said, "When you're leaving on a motor trip to go to the Pacific Northwest and you're living in Santa Ana, you leave early in the morning. You drive to San Francisco or Sacramento and stay there the first night. You don't drive into a motel in Santa Monica as the first stopping place."

"But what could he possibly have to do with anything connected with Marilyn Chelan?" Elsie asked. "Good heavens, he was a top-flight financier, according to the account in the paper. He left two children, a boy nineteen, a girl seventeen. He was actively identified with church work, president of the Chamber of Commerce, and his wife was president of the local women's club."

"I know," I said. "It doesn't make sense. Just the same, give me a pair of scissors, Elsie, and I'll save this clipping."

I cut out the newspaper account of Gillett's untimely demise, folded it, put it in my wallet and rang up the Yellow Cab Company.

"This is Humperhill of the Ventura *Chronicle*," I said. "We're running a story on the murder of Jeanette Latty. We understand that one of your cabdrivers took a suspect out to the Latty residence at about the time the murder was committed. We want to get his name and the number of the cab and, if possible, a photograph."

The woman who was taking the calls was sick and tired of the whole business. "I wish you newspaper people would realize that we're not an information bur—"

"Tut-tut, sister," I said. "You want the right kind of publicity. After all, the business you're in, you need good public relations. What's the guy's name and number?"

"Hermann Oakley," she said. "Cab number 687-J. He has a cabstand at the Pickerell Apartments. Police picked him up a few minutes ago and drove him to headquarters for an interview. He left his cab at the cabstand at the Pickerell Apartments and will telephone in, reporting for duty, when he gets back on the job. So far, we haven't heard from him.

"Now then, does that give you folks enough to rate us good publicity?"

"The very best," I told her. "We'll comment on the efficiency of the organization, on the manner in which you keep track of the whole network of cabs that are constantly patrolling the city, giving high-class service to people who are confronted with the necessity of getting somewhere in a hurry."

"I'll believe that when I see it," she said. "What paper is it going to be in?"

"Well," I said, "I'm working out of Ventura at the moment, but I'll be sending stuff into the wire services and— Just a minute, Bill, sit down, I'll be right with you . . . Atta girl, thanks a lot. Good-by."

I hung up the receiver.

Chapter 12

I WAITED for nearly an hour at the cabstand at the Pickerell Apartment Hotel until the police car drove up.

Sgt. Sellers and the cabdriver were in the back seat.

Sellers opened the door for him.

"All right," I heard him say, "we'll try to make this as painless as possible for you. You'll have to talk once more with the D.A., but that shouldn't take long."

The cabdriver said something that I didn't get, and then Sellers drove away and the driver went over, climbed in his cab, picked up the microphone and reported to cab headquarters that he was back in service.

I gave him about two minutes before I came sauntering along.

I climbed in the cab and gave him an address that would take about fifteen minutes.

"My gosh," I said, "you're good to yourself on a coffee break. I came by earlier and your cab was standing there, dark and deserted. I went and had a cup of coffee myself and—"

"You know where I was?" he asked.

"Sure," I said, "having some coffee and ham and eggs, and maybe a little snooze."

"Snooze my eye!" he said. "The cops had me."

"The hell!"

"That's right."

"What have *you* been doing?"

"Nothing that *I've* been doing, just driving a cab. Some jane had me drive out to a place where a woman got knocked off, and the cops wanted me to make an identification."

"Could you?" I asked.

"Sure."

"Line-up?"

"Oh, the usual thing," he said, grinning. "They put her in a line-up but they saw I had a look at her before she ever got in the line-up. They're sure clever that way. They let you get a glimpse of the person you're supposed to identify, and then later on you see that person in the line-up."

"You've evidently gone through that before."

"Half a dozen times," he said. "Oh, maybe not that many, but it seems like it. We cabdrivers who are on the late night shift get in lots of adventures. I've been held up a couple of times and had to identify the guys that did the holdup, and once I had to identify a guy that put a gun in my back and made me drive like hell, trying to make a getaway. But the cop cars were geared up faster and they closed in on us without any trouble."

"You're sure about tonight, about the girl?" I asked.

"Oh, sure," he said. "I didn't need any line-up. Hell, she asked for me by name."

"How come?"

"Oh," he said, "we get to know some of these gals that are on the make and they like a driver that they know is safe. Word gets passed around that some of us drivers are okay. This girl rang up and asked for Hermann, wanted to know if I was anywhere in the vicinity and free to go— At that, she beat me out of the fare."

"You'd taken her before?"

"Sure," he said. "I'd taken her out to that same address before. I— Say, what the hell!"

A police car glided up behind us, a red spotlight flooded the left side of the car with brilliance, and Oakley pulled in to the curb.

"Now what?" he asked.

The guy who was driving the police car parked it alongside and Frank Sellers got out.

"Well, well, well," he said, "Pint Size himself, trying to pull a smart trick. You know, I just had an idea you might be hanging around, trying to upset the apple cart.

"Get out," Sellers said.

"What's the idea? I've taken a cab and—"

"Get out."

"Now look," I told him, "I—"

Sellers jerked the door open, grabbed the lapel of my coat, nearly tore the garment off yanking me out of the car.

"How much is on the meter, Hermann?" he asked.

"Only a dollar-ten so far."

"A round-trip will be two-twenty," Sellers said, "and a thirty-cent tip will make it two-fifty. Give the guy two-fifty, Pint Size."

"Now look," I told him, "you have no right to—"

Sellers' open hand hit me on the side of the head.

"Give the guy two and a half," he said.

I gave the cabdriver two and a half.

"Get started," Sellers told Oakley, "and don't talk to this guy any more—he's poison."

Sellers waited until the cab had driven away, then looked me over and said, "I should give you a hell of a good working over. You just can't keep your nose out of other people's business."

Sellers looked up and down the deserted street.

I knew what was coming. I had to talk fast to keep from getting a working over.

I said, "If you'd let me tell you what *I* know once in a while, or be willing to listen, you might do better on solving murder cases."

"Listen to what?" he asked.

"To me."

Sellers hesitated for just a second or two, then said, "All right, Pint Size, start talking. It had better be good. When you get all done, I'll start teaching you a lesson about interfering with police investigations."

I said, "We were called in to do a job on Marilyn Chelan as bodyguards. She was our client. The guy only paid the bill."

"I know."

"Bertha got drugged and—"

"For God's sake, Pint Size, tell me something new. Don't try to bamboozle me with a lot of stuff I know already."

104

I said, "The man that hired us was a fellow named Jarvis C. Archer, who is an executive in the steel research company Marilyn was working for."

"I know, I know," he said.

"All right, here's what you *don't* know. Archer was the one who put in those threatening telephone calls and the one who sent those special delivery letters."

"Of course he was," Sellers said. "He had to be. He was in on the deal so that this babe could get herself an alibi. I know it, but I can't prove it."

"With me, you can prove it."

"How?"

I said, "I shadowed Archer after he left the place last night. He went to two telephone booths and put in calls. I had my watch synchronized with standard time on the telephone signal. I made note of the times.

"After those phone calls came in, Bertha telephoned the time service and got the exact time on tape recorder. The times match, right down to the seconds."

"You couldn't see the numbers Archer was calling."

"No, but I didn't have to. Those two calls were received at the exact moment that I timed him placing calls in two different telephone booths."

"And you were tailing Archer?"

"Yes."

"Why?"

"Because I thought it was probably a frame-up job, the way he was acting and the way they'd change the telephone number, get a new unlisted number and the calls would keep right on coming in. She must have told Archer the new telephone number every time and—"

"That's no news," Sellers said. "She and Archer were both playing it hand and glove. Before we get done with her, she'll crack up and implicate him in the murder. She wasn't one damned bit worried about those telephone calls or those letters. That was all an act she was putting on for you and Bertha so she could have a framed-up alibi."

"I don't think so," I said. "I—"

"Well, *I* think so," Sellers said. "Now, wait a minute. You were tailing this guy, Archer?"

"That's right."

"And you ran into the squad car down there on Rhoda Avenue?"

"They ran into me."

"Then Archer was the guy you were tailing," Sellers said. "Archer was the car that went on down there, scouting to see if the coast was clear."

"I can't swear to it. I lost the car I was tailing and then—"

"Don't kid me," Sellers said. "You were tailing that car and you weren't going to let it get away from you. . . . Come on, Pint Size, you've talked your way out of being worked over, but you haven't sold me anything yet. However, if you can testify as to the time of those calls and they check out on the tape recorder, you've given me something I need. . . . Get in."

"Where are we going?" I asked.

"You have one guess."

"Archer?" I asked.

Sellers grinned.

He opened the car door, all but pushed me in, climbed in beside me, slammed the door and said to the driver, "Let's go."

Chapter 13

FRANK SELLERS used the car radio to communicate with the police dispatcher's office and, through them, learned the address of Jarvis C. Archer.

That address proved to be a modern residential address, and Archer's house was designed for modern living. Lots of glass, big, sliding windows and a design which indicated every inch of area had been converted into utility.

Lights were on in the house.

Sellers said, "Come on, Pint Size, this is going to be your party. And if I come out at the bottom of the heap, heaven help you."

We walked up the steps and rang the bell.

The woman who answered the door was somewhere in her thirties, and a raving beauty. She had large eyes, dimples, full lips which gave her an expressive mouth, and long eyelashes.

She was dressed for an evening at home, black velvet toreador pants which accented her curves, a gold lamé overblouse, high-heeled gold slippers, and long, exotic earrings which brushed her throat as she moved.

"Yes?" she asked, standing there with the door thrown open, completely poised and very sure of herself.

Sellers said, "Police, ma'am. We want to talk with Jarvis C. Archer. Does he live here?"

"Yes."

"Is he home?"

"Yes."

"You Mrs. Archer?"

She smiled then and emphasized the dimples.

"I am."

"All right, let me tell you one thing," Sellers said, pulling the soggy cigar out of his mouth to use as a pointer in stabbing the words at her to give them additional emphasis. "Don't ever open the door on a ring after dark and stand there like that. Put a safety chain on that door, open it to the end of the safety chain, find out who's ringing your doorbell and what they want, and if it's someone who tells you he's had trouble with an automobile and wants to get in to use the phone, tell him to give you the number he wants to call and you'll put through the call for him. Then close the door and leave him standing there while you make the call."

Mrs. Archer laughed and said, "I suppose I shouldn't be so—well, fearless isn't the name for it—but I suppose I shouldn't have so little apprehension. Do come in. You say you're the police?"

"These are my credentials," Sellers said, opening the

107

leather wallet he took from his pocket. "Sergeant Frank Sellers. And this is Donald Lam, a private detective."

"Right this way, please."

She ushered us through a little reception hallway into a living room which was furnished for comfort, with a big television, hi-fi, comfortable chairs, a card table with two decks of cards on it.

Archer had been watching television. He evidently hadn't heard us come in.

"Dear," Mrs. Archer said, "here are some people to see you."

Archer jerked his head back with surprise, saw me, frowned portentously, jumped to his feet and said, "Lam, what the devil!"

Sellers stepped forward, pushed out the worn leather wallet with the police star and his I.D. card.

"Police," he said. "I'm Sergeant Frank Sellers. We want to talk with you."

"Well, go ahead and talk," Archer said irritably. "Wouldn't this have kept until tomorrow?"

"No."

"All right, what is it?"

Sellers looked meaningly at Mrs. Archer and coughed.

"Go right ahead," Archer said. "I have no secrets from my wife."

"This is rather a personal matter," Sellers said. "We thought perhaps—"

"Well, quit thinking that way," Archer said. "Let's get it over with. I'm watching an interesting program and, to my knowledge, I have no information that would be of any value to the police in connection with any matter."

Sellers said, "Now listen, if this is a bluff, I'm going to call it, so don't try to make a grandstand now and then scream bloody murder after I spill the beans."

Archer said, "I told you to go ahead."

"All right," Sellers said. "You hired Donald Lam here and his partner, Bertha Cool, to ride herd on a girl who was employed as a secretary in your office."

"What of it?"

"You told them you wanted them to act as bodyguards, you wanted to protect her."

"That's right."

Mrs. Archer smiled and dimpled at Sellers. "I know all about it, Sergeant," she said.

Sellers looked surprised.

"All right," Sellers said, "I'll go on. This girl was receiving anonymous threats through the mail, letters that had been made out of words cut from newspapers and pasted together. She was also getting telephone calls. People would call her on the phone. She'd pick up the receiver, say hello, and the person at the other end of the line wouldn't say anything, just remain on the line, breathing heavily."

"Okay, okay," Archer said. "You know that and I know it so why waste time talking about it? Why are you here?"

"You told Lam and Bertha Cool you'd pay the bill for their services personally."

"Certainly I did," Archer said. "I intend to pass it on to the company as an expense account, but I'm going to do it at my own time and in my own way, so that it doesn't show on its face that I've been hiring a firm of detectives to protect one favorite employee and have everybody in the whole accounting department giving me sideways glances every time I walk by.

"After all, Sergeant, I'm a happily married man, I'm an executive in the company and I don't have to account to every hireling for everything I do. Nor do I care to have them gossiping about my business."

Sellers looked at me and was plainly nonplused.

I said, "The numbers were changed from time to time, and Miss Chelan was given a new unlisted number, but that didn't seem to have the slightest effect on the telephone calls. They came in just the same."

"That's right," Archer said. "And, for your information, Lam, I don't like the idea of you taking on a private job and then running to the police and blabbing all your troubles to them.

"You were hired to find out who was doing what and put a stop to it, and your firm didn't stand out with any great

109

amount of brilliance, if you want my opinion. Anyway, Miss Chelan didn't think you were doing a damned bit of good. You were forcing her to live like a goldfish and she wanted you fired, so you were fired."

"Okay," I said. "For your information, I didn't go to the police, they came to me."

"That's a likely story," Archer said. "How the hell would they know anything about all this, so they could come to you? You're the one that went to them."

Sellers said, "He's giving you the straight goods, Archer. We went to him."

"Why?" Archer asked.

"Let him tell you," Sellers said. "Go ahead, Pint Size, it's your party now. Do the talking."

I said, "I'll begin at the beginning, Archer. Last night, you left Marilyn Chelan's apartment about nine-twenty-five—right?"

"I guess so, I didn't notice the time. I talked with Marilyn and with Bertha Cool, who was there, and gave Mrs. Cool some instructions and tried to cheer Marilyn up a little bit."

"And then," I said, "you drove to a cocktail lounge and had a chat with a friend and a couple of drinks."

"Only one drink," he said. "So it was you, eh?"

"What was?"

"The guy who was trying to tail me."

"That's right. And then you went to a telephone booth and you put through a call that terminated at ten-oh-seven. Then you went to another telephone booth and put through a call that was finished at ten-sixteen. Now, those calls were both to Marilyn Chelan's new unlisted number, and when you had her on the line, you didn't say a word but just started breathing heavily."

Archer threw back his head and laughed.

"Care to deny it?" I asked.

"Hell, no," he said. "Why *should* I deny it? I was testing out my new service. When you buy a tape recorder, you test it out. When you have a new telephone installed, you call a friend to see how it's working. I'd got a new detective agency on the job and I felt I'd test you out a little bit and see what your technique was."

"Then you claim now that you weren't the person who had been sending the special delivery letters and making the other telephone calls?"

"I sent the last two special delivery letters," he said. Chopped the words out of the newspaper and pasted it together myself. That was another effort on my part to see how efficient you people were going to be. I bought a rubber type printing press and set up the address. And I may say that there was nothing you did that impressed me that you had any great amount of brilliance, as far as a detective agency was concerned. Although I will admit that the idea of shadowing me was a good one. . . . I take it, you wanted to see if it was what you call an inside job?"

"That's right."

"Well, I was testing. I wanted to find out a few things myself. So, okay, we were both a little suspicious of each other."

"And then," I said, "you took off and drove down to Rhoda Avenue, you started to turn in at 762, then saw something that made you change your mind, and you went away from there fast and then resorted to evasive tactics to make sure you couldn't be followed."

He looked at me with sheer surprise stamped on his countenance.

"762 Rhoda Avenue? What the hell are you talking about?"

"That's where you went after the telephone calls."

"Guess again," he said. "After that second telephone call, I did a lot of thinking. I had been feeling that someone was following me and I got sure of it driving down the boulevard. I kept looking in my rearview mirror and finally got this car spotted. So I charged into a group of cars that were bunched together, went on past them, saw that one was a car very similar to the car I was driving, went in front of it and then made a sudden right turn without giving any signal on the blinker light and without putting on my brakes."

"Then what did you do?" I asked.

"Then," he said, "I drove around the block and waited to

see if someone came driving up. I thought perhaps the same people that were giving Marilyn a bad time would try to make something of it as far as I was concerned, and I decided we'd have it out."

"Just you, yourself, against an undetermined number of people?"

"That's right," he said. "I had with me what is known as an equalizer."

"Got a permit?" Sellers asked.

"Sure," Archer said. "In my business, I carry large sums of money at times and the police were only too glad to give me a permit. They found out I know how to use a gun, and when the officer gave me the gun, he told me that he hoped I was held up and had the guts and the skill to make one less bandit in the city."

Sellers said, "You know a Jeanette Latty?"

"Latty . . . Latty . . ." Archer said. "I've heard the name or read it, but I'm damned if I know where."

"*I* know her," Mrs. Archer said.

"You do!" Sellers exclaimed in surprise.

"Why, certainly. I think you know her, too, Jarvis. I introduced you one night at a cocktail lounge."

"How long have you known her?" Sellers asked Mrs. Archer.

"Quite a while. She's an old friend," Mrs. Archer said. "She worked in the same office I did, back before I was married. And then we got the idea of coming to Hollywood and crashing the pictures, and we pooled our resources and came here by bus."

"And then what?" Sllers asked.

"Well, we kept together for a while, but I sized up the situation and decided that it took more than a figure, a personality and a few other things to crash the gates of the studios to any advantage, so I started looking around for a job, and that's where I met Jarvis. We went together for two or three months and then got married."

"But you didn't go out at all with Jeanette Latty and your husband on foursomes?"

"Heavens, no. Jeanette is— Well, she's an awfully nice

112

girl, but she's different. She's— Well, I don't want to say anything that would sound catty, and I can't say what I want to say without it sounding catty. But she's not the type that Jarvis would go for. In fact, he would be a little uneasy if she were in the party."

"When did you see her last?" Sellers asked.

"Why? What's she have to do with all this?"

"She lives on Rhoda Avenue," Sellers said.

"That's right, she does," Mrs. Archer said. "I remember now, that's her new address. She's been there for a while. I haven't seen her in ages, but she's a great one to telephone. We talk on the phone more or less frequently. She knows she wouldn't fit in with my husband, so she does her visiting by telephone."

"Jeanette didn't get a job?" Sellers asked.

"No. Jeanette had had a taste of meat. She wasn't going back to milk. She tried waiting tables in a place where the tables in any one of the Hollywood restaurants and no one a dime a dozen in Hollywood.

"Honestly, I believe you could take the ranking star of the moment, the one who is considered the very hottest sex pot in Hollywood, put a uniform on her and put her waiting tables in any one of the Hollywood restaurants and no one would even notice her. Directors, producers, scouts would sit at the table and talk about someone who had won a beauty contest back in Joplin, Missouri, or Kalamazoo, Michigan, but wouldn't even notice the girl who was waiting on them except to bawl her out if she didn't keep the coffee cups filled."

"So then what?"

"Well, Jeanette and I drifted apart. She went into various things."

"Call girl?" Frank Sellers asked.

"Good heavens, no! Not Jeanette! But she did get this idea for some kind of a hostess service, and I think she had a dream of getting into the travel agency business, personally escorted tours and things of that sort. I haven't kept up with her too much."

"When was the last time you saw her?"

113

"Good heavens, I don't know. It's been quite a while."

"Really, Sergeant," Archer said, "this inquiry is getting a little bit out of hand. It seems to me that you're prying unnecessarily into my wife's personal life and background."

"For your information," Sellers said, "your friend, Jeanette Latty, was murdered sometime between ten last night and three this morning."

Mrs. Archer looked at him wide-eyed for a moment, then said, "No, oh, *no!*"

"It happens that I'm dealing with facts," Sellers said. "That's the basis of my interest. Now then, when was the last time you saw Jeanette Latty?"

Mrs. Archer made a fist out of her hand, pressed the white knuckles against her lower lip.

If she was putting on an act, it was a hell of a good act.

"The last time you saw her," Sellers said.

She said, in a small, weak voice, "I saw her . . . two or three nights ago. I ran in to her accidentally, and we had drinks together."

"That was the last time you saw her?"

"Yes."

"Where were you last night?"

"Home."

"Any way of proving it?"

"It depends on what part of the night you're talking about. My husband was out until quite late, and after a woman gets married, her husband is virtually the only person she can call on to say where she spends her evenings—and nights."

"What time did you get home?" Sellers asked Archer.

"It was after midnight. I didn't look at my watch."

"Where was your wife?"

"In bed, asleep."

"Did you ask him where he'd been?" Sellers asked Mrs. Archer.

"No. I *never* ask him where he's been. I never ask him to account to me for his time or his acquaintances."

"He's gone quite a bit of the time?" Sellers asked.

"Of course he is. He has customers to entertain, and when he's entertaining customers, Sergeant, I assume that there's a certain amount of conviviality and I assume that there are women in the party. I just don't ask questions."

"You mean you don't care?"

"I feel that marriage is what you make it. Any woman continues to be in competition with every other woman in the world. Any time I can't give my husband more than any other woman can give him, I expect to lose him. That doesn't mean that he isn't going to look around and it doesn't mean that he isn't going to sample merchandise. It also doesn't mean that he isn't going to strut his stuff as a salesman when he gets around some good-looking cutie who is making passes at him.

"There are some things I don't like about my husband's business life, about the exposure to temptation and the entertaining he has to do, but that's a part of his life, it's a part of his career. I put up with it. I don't ask questions and I don't care to have you do so in my presence. So if you're going to question him any more about last night, I'll leave the room—provided, of course, you're finished with me."

Sellers was thoughtful. "I guess I'm finished with both of you. I'm sorry I had to barge in on you in this way, but, after all, we're investigating a murder. And the fact that your husband employed a firm of private detectives to try and find out who was threatening his secretary—"

"Has nothing whatever to do with the case you're investigating," Archer interpolated.

"Probably not," Sellers said.

"Where is Marilyn now?" Archer asked.

"I'm sure I can't tell you right at this moment," Sellers said. "We questioned her earlier in the evening, and we may question her again."

"Well, I'd like to see her," Archer said. "I don't like the idea of any publicity in connection with what I did. I'm counting on you, Sergeant, to see to it that my name is not connected with any publicity, particularly publicity that would involve the corporation by which I am employed. That would cause very grave repercussions—very grave repercussions, indeed, Sergeant. . . . I think you'll find it will pay to consider my wishes. You'll find I have very powerful friends."

"I'm just asking questions at the moment," Sellers said. "You'll notice I've got no newspaper reporters along, and I came to your home to ask the questions instead of asking you to come down to headquarters, where newspaper reporters might be hanging out, catch the license numbers on your automobile and ask you about what was going on.

"Now then," Sellers went on, "I want to use your telephone and then I'll be gone."

Mrs. Archer said, "This way, please," and led him over to a little telephone stand in the hallway.

"I can get outside on this?" he asked.

"Yes, it's all connected."

Sellers dialed a number, said "Hello, Frank Sellers talking. Let me talk with Code, will you?"

A moment later he said, "Sellers. What have you found out?"

There was silence for a moment, then Sellers said, "Read them again, will you?"

Sellers pulled a notebook from his pocket, started taking notes.

There was an uncomfortable two or three minutes. Finally, Archer said, "Perhaps I misjudged the situation after all, Lam. I hope I can trust to *your* discretion."

"We try to be discreet," I said, "but, in a case of this sort, we can't give the police false information and we can't withhold information which might lead to the solution of a murder."

Mrs. Archer said, "Well, whoever it was who murdered poor Jeanette, I certainly hope they get him and make him pay the penalty."

She turned to her husband. "Where's Marilyn now, Jarvis?"

"I don't know," he said.

"You don't need to hold out on me, Jarvis. You understand that."

"I know, Dawn, honey, but I'm telling you the truth. She hasn't communicated with me. I'm hoping that she will before very long, because I want to know where she is, and I've

116

got to make some arrangements with the company. I can't just continue giving her an indefinite leave of absence on account of ill health."

Sellers finished his telephone conversation, came back and said, "Well, thanks a lot. I'm sorry I bothered you folks, but I wanted to get this situation cleared up. Come on, Lam, let's go."

"There's nothing else we can do? No further information we can give?" Archer asked.

"That depends," Sellers said, eyeing him narrowly. "If you've got any further information, you can sure give it to me."

"I haven't any."

"You've told me all you know?"

"Yes."

"And you?" he asked Mrs. Archer.

She nodded her head.

"Then there's no further information I can get here," Sellers said, smiling in a friendly way. "Thanks a lot."

Archer escorted us to the door. "No hard feelings," he said.

"Sure not," Sellers agreed.

Archer looked at me. "No hard feelings, Lam."

"No hard feelings," I told him.

We got out in the police car. I said to Sellers, "Well, you certainly backed off awfully fast from that one."

Sellers threw the soggy stogy out of the car widow, spat explosively, said, "Dammit, Lam, you steered me into a mare's nest."

"What do you mean?" I asked.

"What do I mean!" Sellers exploded. "We're hitting this thing right on the nerve, and we can't let them find out."

"You think Archer killed her?" I asked.

"Probably his wife," Sellers said. "Hell's bells! Don't you get the sketch?"

"I'm dumb," I told him.

"Any old time," Sellers said, and was silent for a few moments.

"Where to?" the driver asked.

"Take Lam back and we'll drop him off," Sellers said.

We rode in silence for a while, then Sellers said, "Now look, Pint Size, I've got to tell you this much because I don't want you to upset the apple cart. Dawn Archer was one of Jeanette Latty's escort girls."

"You're sure?"

"Of course I'm sure. We had a little notebook that we found in Jeanette Latty's dresser drawer. It had a series of numbers in it. We couldn't figure out what those numbers were, so we turned them over to the code department. The code department tried a lot of different combinations and finally came up with the solution."

"What's the solution?"

"They were telephone numbers."

"Couldn't you tell that without turning it over to the code department?"

"Hell, no," Sellers said. "First, she wrote the numbers backwards, then she put two blind numbers on the front and two blind numbers on the rear, so the middle seven numbers were the only ones that counted. But there were eleven numbers in each column. That's where the code department got the first break. They found that all the numbers were eleven digits and the seventh, eight and ninth numbers had enough similarity so that the code department thought there might be some connection. So they started experimenting, finally decided they might be telephone numbers and that the numbers had been written backwards with two dummy numbers in front and two dummy numbers on the rear. When they tried that out, it clicked.

"Now then, the number of Dawn Archer was one of those numbers. While I was telephoning I noted her number on the telephone and it checked out."

I said, "Mrs. Archer told us that Jeanette Latty telephoned her from time to time."

"How true," Sellers observed dryly.

I said, "Mrs. Archer couldn't afford to be caught in a trap of that sort."

"That's right, Sellers said, "she couldn't afford to be *caught*. She probably went on a special type of party."

"Why? Obviously she didn't need the money."

"She didn't need the money," Sellers said, "but she wanted the excitement and she needed the companionship. Women do strange things when they're beginning to get frustrated."

"You think she was beginning to get frustrated?"

"What the hell," Sellers said. "Use your eyes and ears. Here was Archer staying away from home a lot of the time, doing entertaining, his wife being broadminded about it and telling him not to account to her for what he did with his time, not even turning a hair when she knew that he'd been getting detectives to protect his good-looking secretary from mysterious telephone calls. . . . What the hell!"

"So what do you do now?" I asked.

"What we do," Sellers said, "has no connection with what you do."

"All right, what do I do?" I asked.

"Nothing," he said.

"How about Hermann Oakley, that cabdriver you think he could be mistaken?"

"You're damned right I think he could be mistaken," Sellers said. "For your information, we've had two or three raps on Oakley, and he's trying to curry favor with the department. He thought we wanted him to identify Marilyn Chelan, so he sure as hell identified Marilyn Chelan. But now I'm not so sure. I'm going to have a nice confidential talk with him and see what happens."

"And what about Marilyn Chelan?"

Sellers said, "We're going to let her go, and try to keep her out of the limelight as much as possible. I think we can use her before we get done."

"What do I tell her?" I asked.

"Not a damned thing," he said. And then, after a moment, added, "What are you hanging around her for? Your job is done, you were paid to do a job and you did it. I can't blame you for trying to promote something on the side, but right now that's skating on thin ice."

"I wasn't trying to promote anything," I said. "I was trying to do the job we were hired for."

"You were fired."

"Before the job was done," I said. "I still had some time to put in on it."

"All right, that time is used up now," Sellers said. "Just keep your nose clean on this thing and don't tip my hand."

I said, "All right, this is your baby, but I think it's growing pretty fast."

"What do you mean by that?"

"I'm not entirely sold."

"Hell, I'm not trying to sell you," Sellers said. "I'm just trying to get you to back away from this thing and leave me in the driver's seat."

The driver pulled up in front of the place where I'd told them the agency car was parked. "This okay?" he asked.

"This is okay," Sellers said. "Out and on your way, Pint Size, and say nothing about any of this."

Chapter 14

I WAITED until the police car had rounded the corner, then started my car and drove to Santa Ana.

The Gillett house was a veritable mansion. Several cars were parked around it.

I rang the bell.

A maid came to the door.

"I'm sorry to disturb her," I said, "but I have to see Mrs. Gillett on a matter of the greatest importance."

"Who are you?"

I said, "The name will mean nothing to her, but if you will tell her that my business has to do with the vacation she and her husband were about to take, I think she will understand."

The maid said, "Just a minute," closed the door and left me standing there while she went inside.

A few moments later the door was opened and a big, steely-eyed individual with bushy eyebrows took over.

"All right," he said, "what's the pitch?"

"May I ask who you are?"

"I'm a friend of the family, and I'm asking who you are."

I said, "I have a message for Mrs. Gillett."

"You should know she can't see anyone," the man said.

"It would be a lot better if she saw me. Just tell her that my business has to do with the vacation she and her husband were about to take, and I am trying to save her money, notoriety and a lot of mental anguish."

"Give me your name," he said.

I said, "I'll give you my name if it can be kept in confidence."

"I'm not making any promises."

I said, "You're a friend of the family?"

"Yes."

I handed him one of my cards. "My name is Donald Lam. I'm a private detective and I'm doing this on my own. I'm trying to help, not trying to hinder. But unless something is done within the next twenty-four hours, it's going to be too late."

"Too late for what?"

"Too late to antidote the poison," I said.

"What poison?"

"The poison she's being forced to take."

"You talk in circles," he said.

"A circle," I said, "has one distinctive characteristic—all of its parts are equidistant from the center."

"Come in," he invited.

He escorted me into a hushed house and into a living room. "Sit there," he said.

He left the room and was back in about two minutes.

"Come with me."

He led the way to an upstairs suite. There was a sitting room fitted with big easy chairs, a desk, a telephone and a door, apparently leading into sleeping quarters.

"Sit down, Lam," he said.

121

A few moments later, the door from the sleeping quarters opened and an attractive, dignified woman entered.

She was wearing a housecoat and slippers. Her face was as much without expression as though it had been carved from stone.

The man said, "I'm Norman Clinton. I'm a friend of the family. This is Mrs. Gillett. Now then, you've made some cryptic remarks about circles. I'm going to ask you to cut right to the center."

"I'd like to see Mrs. Gillett alone."

"You can't," he said. "Any business that you have with her can be shared with me. For your information, I am the executor named in Baxter Gillett's will."

I looked at Mrs. Gillett.

"Have you paid any blackmail yet?" I asked.

Her face remained utterly without expression.

Clinton frowned and said, "Now, that's exactly the type of gambit I was afraid you were going to try. I suppose you want to get a job for your detective agency. Well, I can tell you here and now that you're out of luck and I'm sorry I disturbed Mrs. Gillett on the strength of your rather cryptic utterances."

I said, "If she hasn't paid blackmail, she's going to have to, unless she does certain things."

"What things?" he asked.

"Either tell the truth," I said, "or fix it so the truth can never be discovered."

"What do you mean by truth?"

I said, "This vacation business is thoroughly, utterly, absolutely cockeyed. When people leave on a vacation, they pack a lot of suitcases, they load up the car with golf clubs, fishing tackle or whatever else they have in the way of a hobby. They start out early in the morning and they drive—"

"This was a different vacation," he said. "Baxter Gillett was a very busy man. He was held here until the close of the stock market, then he had some matters to transact, and, all in all, he couldn't get away before night."

I said, "All right, if that's your story and you want to

stick to it, that's fine. But if you haven't paid blackmail yet, you will.

"Baxter Gillett was having an evening on the town. He was in a motel with a woman. He had a heart attack and died. The woman ducked out but was sport enough to telephone the family to tell what had really happened.

"You people had a quick meeting. You decided that the family couldn't stand that sort of scandal, particularly since you were living in a community the size of Santa Ana, and with the temperament and background of the associates Baxter Gillett had made in his lifetime.

"So some friend of the family—probably you—got busy and Mrs. Gillett went in to the motel and the next morning reported her husband's death."

Clinton got up out of the chair and said, "I should smash your face in for being the dirty rotter that you are."

Mrs. Gillett spoke for the first time. She said, "Wait a minute, Norman."

She turned to me. "What makes you think all this is true?" she asked.

"Because," I told her, "I think your husband knew a woman by the name of Jeanette Latty, who ran a so-called escort service, providing escorts for out-of-town businessmen who wanted entertainment.

"For your information, Jeanette Latty was murdered sometime between ten o'clock last night and three o'clock this morning.

"If you start paying blackmail, there's no end to it. If you're being blackmailed, or if anyone attempts blackmail, there's only one way to handle it."

"How's that?" Clinton asked.

"You nail the blackmailer to a cross," I said.

"And how can that be done?"

"There are several ways."

"Outside of going to the police, I know of no way," Clinton said.

"Perhaps *you* don't," I said. "I do."

"How do I know that *you're* not the one who is trying and has been trying blackmail?"

"You don't," I said, "except that I've come out in the open and given you my name and put my reputation and my license as a private detective on the line."

"Why are you here?"

"Because I admire courage, because I want to help, and because I think the only way I can keep an innocent party from being framed for the murder of Jeanette Latty is to have your help."

"And, in return for our help, what are you prepared to give?"

"My help."

"That's a dubious quantity," he said.

"All right," I told him. "I couldn't do any more than make the offer."

I got up as though preparing to go.

Clinton exchanged glances with Mrs. Gillett. "Sit down," he said, in the voice of one who is accustomed to giving orders and expects to have them obeyed.

I sat down.

Clinton said, "Wait there."

He nodded to Mrs. Gillett and they went through the door into the bedroom. They were gone about ten minutes. When they came back, Clinton said, "I've had quite a time looking you up. The police say you're honest but daring and unconventional, and, from time to time, you're in hot water."

I said, "You evidently have good connections."

"I have," Clinton said dryly.

He looked at Mrs. Gillett.

She said, "Mr. Lam, I'm going to put the cards on the table and I'm going to confide in you. The step I am taking is the result of my own decision, predicated upon the impression you have made on me. . . . Call it a woman's intuition, if you want to."

I simply nodded.

"And," she said, "I may say, it is against the advice of Norman Clinton, who feels that I should wait before I do anything. But I somehow have the distinct feeling that you are honest and fair. I don't know all of your motivations, but

I don't think you'd approach me in this manner and then betray my interest."

I said, "I'm trying to get at certain facts."

"All right," she said, "I'll give you the facts in a nutshell.

"My husband and I have two children. One is a boy nineteen years old, the other is a girl seventeen years old. Because of my husband's status in the community, they have a certain amount of social position. To have these children involved in scandal at the present time would be unthinkable.

"The girl, in particular, is entering upon a social life which, of course, means a great deal to her.

"I have long been aware that my husband was not a saint. I doubt if very many husbands are. I know that he made business trips and I had reason to believe that on some of those trips he engaged in extramarital activities.

"I don't think he did this because he loved me or his family any the less, but simply because he was a strong, virile man who enjoyed a good time, and when he was away from home, he and his men friends were swept along, so to speak, on a tide of devil-may-care activity.

"Under those circumstances, when a good-looking, virile man meets a girl who, for reasons of her own, is willing to submit to him and leads him on with conversation and gestures which are flattering to the male ego, I feel that the result is more or less inevitable.

"This is probably an unconventional way for a wife to talk and a shocking way for a widow to talk, but I want you to know the facts."

Again I nodded.

"On the night of the fourth," she said, "at eleven-fifteen, I received a telephone call. The person making the call was a woman, simply a feminine voice. The voice was rather seductive, wasn't particularly harsh or coarse, but, under the circumstances, very businesslike.

"This woman asked if I was Mrs. Baxter C. Gillett and I told her I was. She said, 'Listen carefully because I can't repeat. I'm at the Skyview Motel at Santa Monica. I went here with your husband. We checked in about half an hour ago.

" 'Somewhat to my surprise, your husband checked in under his own name, probably because he was driving his own car and the man who was managing the motel insisted on looking at the license number and writing it down.

" 'We had a few drinks and went to bed. Your husband had a heart attack and is dead. I have listened carefully for a heartbeat, I have felt for a pulse. There is none.

" 'In order to protect myself, I am getting out.

" 'I am giving you this notice so that you can do whatever you need to protect yourself and your family. I realize from what I know of your husband that you have a social position which should be protected, and you can count on my discretion if you want to do something to protect yourself.

" 'The motel unit is number fourteen. I am leaving, locking the door, but leaving the key under the doormat. You will find it there in case you wish to do anything about it before the authorities are notified.'

"With that, the woman hung up."

"What did you do?" I asked.

She said, "I called Norman Clinton. I told him the whole story. He decided that the best thing to do would be to investigate, and if there was any truth in the story, to take steps to protect the family good name.

"So we packed up some suitcases as though going on a vacation. Norman drove me to the motel, I found the key under the doormat and we went into the unit. My husband was lying there, nude in bed and dead."

"Go on," I said.

"I realized that I had a joint responsibility. I was a wife, but I was also a mother. Because I had to do what had to be done, I sat up during the night, then in the morning I put on pajamas and a robe and frantically called the office of the motel, asking for a doctor.

"The manager came down to see what the trouble was all about, and, fortunately, took me for granted.

"Apparently my husband had been the one to sign the register and the manager had had no particular reason to notice his companion.

126

"I said that we were starting on a vacation, that we had left in the evening so that we wouldn't be detained by any early morning emergencies or telephone calls, that I had been nervous from the problems incident to packing and getting away, that I had taken a sleeping pill, had gone to sleep and had awakened at seven in the morning.

"A doctor was summoned, he pronounced my husband dead, the coroner's office was notified, and, after listening to my story, decided there would be no necessity for an inquest, that death had undoubtedly been due to a heart attack.

"I returned home and carried through the act.

"Yesterday morning I received a mysterious telephone call from a woman. I have no idea who she was. I am, however, quite certain it wasn't the same one who had called to tell me my husband was dead. That woman had a throaty, rather seductive voice. This woman who called yesterday morning had a close-clipped, businesslike voice. It was crisp and just a little harsh.

"She said, 'I'm sorry that I have to do this, but I have no other alternative. I am desperately in need of five hundred dollars, in cash. I know all about the true facts surrounding your husband's death, I know who the woman in the case is, and unless I receive five hundred dollars in cash before two o'clock this afternoon, I will have to make the money I need by telling what I know to the newspapers. I can get at least twice the amount I need by telling my story to a newspaper reporter I know, who would love to make a big headline scandal out of it.'

"The woman went on to say that I should listen carefully because she wouldn't call again, that I was to take five hundred dollars, put it in a plain envelope, drive out to a certain intersection, turn left, that at exactly three-tenths of a mile from the intersection there would be an orange grove and a mailbox by the side of the road, that I was to put the envelope on top of the mailbox and drive on without looking back.

"She went on to say that if I would comply with her instructions, she would protect my confidence, that the five hundred dollars was all she needed to tide her over, that she regretted very much having to do this but she was desperate, that if she didn't have the five hundred dollars it would mean a very great personal tragedy to her.

"Then she hung up."

"You got the five hundred dollars and did as she requested?"

"Yes."

"You made no attempt to find out who the woman was or when she took the money?"

"No. She had warned me that any attempt to do that would result in the very publicity I wished to avoid. She pointed out that if I managed to outwit her and she was arrested on a charge of extortion, that her arrest would bring about the very publicity we were trying to avoid."

Mrs. Gillett stopped talking and looked at Clinton, as though she wanted his approval for the way she had put the cards on the table. But Clinton was staring thoughtfully at the carpet.

"All right," I said, "that's the first bite."

"You think there will be others?"

"Of course, there will be others," I said. "The first bite was simply for the purpose of softening you up. It will probably go along in installments of five hundred dollars for a while, and then there will be an increase. And then they'll tell you that they have to have one big payment in order to enable them to buy a business which will make them independent of all this blackmail, which is as distasteful to them as it is to you. . . . Once these things start, they never stop."

"I had anticipated something like that might happen," she said, "but I also felt that, with the passage of time, it would be difficult for this woman to have a club she could use. The story would no longer be timely and the proof couldn't be produced."

"One other thing," I said. "I take it your husband had lots of business interests?"

"Lots of them."

"A financier?"

"Yes."

"Did he own any stock in the Molybdenum Steel Research Importing Company?"

It was Clinton who answered that question. "I think he had the controlling interest. They were headed for a proxy fight in that company. What do you know about it?"

"Not much," I said. "Did he have any real estate interests? Subdivision financing?"

"Lots of them," Clinton said.

"Do you know a man named George Littleton Dix?"

Clinton thought for a moment, then shook his head.

"A Jarvis C. Archer?"

"Never heard of him."

I got to my feet, said, "Thanks for your confidence. I'm going to try to see that you don't regret it."

"But what do I do," she asked, "if there should be any more requests for payments?"

I said, "Get in touch with me. Don't talk with anyone in the office except me. Here's one of my cards."

She took the card. I handed one to Clinton.

"Did you talk at any length with the manager of the motel?" I asked.

She shook her head. "I avoided him as much as possible. He took it for granted I was the woman with Baxter, and I wanted to keep the situation on that basis."

"Okay," I said. "I'll do what I can to help."

"What," Clinton asked, "are your rates? What kind of a deal can you make with us in a case of this sort?"

"None as yet," I told him. "I'm working on my own right now. I got interested in the case because of activities in connection with another client."

"Would there be any conflict of interests?" Clinton asked. "Anything to prevent you from representing us?"

"No conflict of interests," I told him. "I was fired from the other case. But I don't like to go around soliciting business. I'll just keep plugging away at this thing to gratify my own personal curiosity, if you don't mind."

129

"If you need any money for expenses," he said, "we could—"

"I'll let you know in case I need anything," I told him. "But right at present I'm giving the party."

Chapter 15

WHEN I DROVE UP at my apartment and parked the agency heap in front of my apartment house, a police car was waiting.

One of the officers got out and came over to me.

"Lam?" he asked.

"Right."

"Sergeant Sellers wants to see you."

"I've seen him."

"He wants to see you again."

"I've got things to do, and—"

"Get your car started and follow us."

I got back in the agency car.

The officer at the wheel started the motor. The other one picked up the microphone and reported to the dispatcher that Lam was on his way.

"Follow along behind. Don't try anything," the officer said.

I followed the cruiser.

We went out toward Rhoda Avenue. About two-thirds of the way, another police car pulled alongside. Two cops were in the front seat. Sgt. Sellers was in the back seat.

They flagged me to the curb.

Sellers got out and climbed in with me.

"Keep moving," he said. "Follow that police car in front."

"What's the big idea?" I asked.

"This idea of yours, you were trying to sell me, about Archer being mixed up in this thing," he said.

"Was that my idea?"

"You're damned right it was your idea, and it stinks."

"Why does it stink?"

"Archer is a close friend of one of the members of the police commission. And, boy, did I get *my* ears pinned back. Not only for asking questions that were personal, but taking you along on an official investigation."

"So what do we do now?"

"*We* don't do a damned thing," Sellers said. "*I'm* doing it now."

"Doing what?"

Sellers said, "We've had another talk with that taxi driver. He's told us lots of things he had been trying to hold out on us."

"Things he's just thought of?" I asked.

"Things you won't like," Sellers said. "He saw your agency car parked out there. He says you were signaling Marilyn Chelan. He thinks you picked her up and drove her home."

"He's crazy," I said. "Why didn't he wait?"

"Wait for what?"

"Marilyn, or whoever his passenger was."

"She sent him on a wild-goose chase, that's why. I'll admit I don't like this guy. He tried to hold out on us and I don't like it, but he's caved in now. Jeanette Latty used to try to swing all her taxi business his way. He had a pretty good hunch what was going on. He tried to play innocent when he identified Marilyn the first time. We've got that all out of him. The guy's telling the truth now."

"Second time around, eh?" I asked.

"Keep driving," Sellers said, "*I'll* do the thinking."

We drove for a while in silence, then Sellers said, "You told me that you ducked into a driveway, lay low for a while, then started out trying to get away and blundered right into the patrol car."

"That's right."

"Where did you hide out?"

"The first time was in a driveway. I don't know that I

could give you the address. I probably would know the place when we came to it."

"We'll come to it," Sellers said. Then, after a moment, "Anybody see you there?"

"A man came out in the first driveway I went into. I pretended I was looking for someone. He seemed a little suspicious, so I drove out of there and parked down the street."

"How close to the address on Rhoda Avenue, the one where Jeanette Latty lived?"

"Half a dozen blocks, I guess."

"Not at the mouth of an alley where you could see the Latty house?"

"Hell, no."

"Turn here," Sellers said.

We turned in to Rhoda Avenue.

"Now, show me where you hid out when you had your car parked," Sellers said.

I turned to the right, off Rhoda Avenue, tried a cross street, then said, "I'm not entirely certain. I *think* it was down here in this block, about in the middle— There's the place, right in that driveway."

"That's the place where you got kicked out?"

"That's right."

"And where did you go from there?"

"Let's see," I said. "I went down about half a block and—"

"Keep driving," Sellers said.

I drove down half the block and said, "I think it was here I parked."

"Keep driving," Sellers said.

I drove on until I came back to Rhoda Avenue.

"Turn right," Sellers said.

I turned right.

"Now, turn into this alley."

I turned into the alley.

"Make a U-turn, come back out so you're facing Rhoda Avenue, but don't quite get to the edge of Rhoda Avenue."

I did as he instructed.

"Turn out your lights and shut off your motor," Sellers said.

We sat there for a moment in silence.

Sellers got out and said, "Stay right there until I tell you."

Sellers walked back down the street and over toward the murder house at 762. I could see it from where I was parked. He talked to the men in the police cars. They drove down out of sight.

A taxicab came by, driving slow. It circled the block and came past me again.

The second time it circled the block, Sellers was in it. The cab came to a stop at the mouth of the alley.

Sellers got out, and the driver left the motor running and the lights on, but got out and joined Sellers. They came over to my car.

"This it?" Sellers asked.

The cabdriver looked me over with a steady, insolent appraisal. It was Hermann Oakley.

"It's the same make and model of car," he said, "and I think this is the guy that was in it."

"Wait a minute," I said. "You're all wet. I—"

"Shut up," Sellers said. "I'm doing the talking."

He turned to the cabdriver. "What happened?"

The cabby said, "She got out and went up to the front door. She didn't ring the bell. She— That is, I don't think she did. She hesitated. . . . Then she got out and started walking around the house."

"Then what?"

"Then I saw her shadow at the side door, and the side door opened and I could see her figure in the illumination."

"Did she go in?"

"She went in."

"Then what?"

"She'd told me to drive a block down the street and wait."

"Did you?"

"Yes."

"How long did you wait?"

"She said to wait ten minutes."

"Did you?"

"I waited quite a while—all of fifteen minutes."

"But you drove away without her. Why?"

133

"She walked down to the cab, said she wouldn't need me any more and paid me off."

"Do you know how she got back?"

"The driver of this car picked her up. I saw him signaling her."

"How?"

"Striking matches, or a cigarette lighter."

"How many times?"

"I didn't count—four or five."

"Then what?"

"Before I drove off, I saw her get in the car with him."

"Then what?"

"They drove away."

"When you told your story earlier, you said you didn't get paid off, that you quit waiting."

"I've gone over all that with you, Sergeant. There was a racket here for a taxi driver. I was cashing in on it. This babe was one of the regulars. I didn't know there'd been any murder. I was trying to protect her."

I said, "Just like you're trying to protect yourself now."

"Shut up," Sellers said to me.

"I can't be sure about this guy, but I'm pretty darned certain about the make and model of the car parked here in the alley—and I'm sure as hell certain about the signaling. And I know that when she came out of the house she drove off with him."

I said, "Look, Sellers, I didn't park here. I didn't do any signaling. I didn't pick up Marilyn Chelan or anyone else. But I *did* see a car the same color, the same make and model as this, cruising by slowly. I did see a taxi."

Sellers might not have heard me.

"Take a good look at this guy," Sellers said to the cab-driver.

"I've looked. He's the one who questioned me a while ago."

"You think he's the driver of that car?"

"I'll put it on the line. I can't swear to it. I *know* the car was the same make and model as this. I *think* it was the same car."

"Okay," Sellers said, "that's all. You can go."

Sellers climbed in the car with me. "All right, Pint Size," he said, "back to your apartment, and you can do some talking on the way."

I said, "That cabdriver is crazy as hell."

"I know," Sellers said.

"And that's a hell of a way to make an identification," I said. "You want to identify a person, you put him in a line-up and let—"

"Thanks. Thanks a lot," Sellers said. "I always like to have you gifted amateurs tell us how we should conduct our business.

"Now then, Pint Size, I'm going to give you a break. You're protecting this jane, I don't know why. I'm not saying she was the one who committed the murder and I'm not saying you are. But I'm saying she told you something about this hook-up with Jeanette Latty and you told her something that she could do to protect herself. You went out here to put your plan into operation. She came out here in the cab as soon as Bertha was drugged to sleep. She looked around the house, scouted the place, made sure the thing was okay, the coast was clear, and signaled you. You signaled her back and she let the cab go. Now then, what did you two do?"

I said, "You're all wet."

"I'm giving it to you straight," Sellers said. "You're mixed in this thing right up to your eyebrows, and this is murder, Pint Size. Now, I don't think you're a killer, but you certainly do go overboard for a skirt. This girl told you all about being tangled up in a deal with Jeanette Latty and you worked out a plan to unscramble things and get her off the hook and all square with Archer. Now then, somewhere along the line things went sour and Jeanette Latty got bumped off.

"I'm not saying *you* did it—not yet.

"I am saying, however, that Marilyn Chelan scouted the premises, and then you and Marilyn started putting some kind of a plan into operation. Now then, we want to know what that plan was, and we want to know fast."

"I tell you, you're all wet. I wasn't parked there at all."

135

"Hermann Oakley, the cabdriver, says you were. You heard him."

"I heard him," I said.

"So," Sellers said, "you come up with all this cock-and-bull story about Archer wanting to get Marilyn Chelan out of town for some reason and all of this elaborate stuff with anonymous telephone calls and threatening letters, and all that stuff."

I said, "You're crazy. This cabdriver is telling you what you want to know, so you listen to him. There are ten thousand cars like this in the city. How the hell could a taxi driver cruising along Rhoda Avenue see a car parked in an alley and recognize the driver? It's a crazy story. I gave you the straight dope, but you found out Archer was a friend of one of the police commissioners and now you're looking for a patsy. You're not going to pin it on me."

"I'm not pinning anything on anybody," Sellers said. "I'm making an investigation. But I'm not going to pull my punches just because I've known you for a while. I know you well enough to know you're quick and sharp and clever and unconventional. If you ask me, it was only a question of time until you got yourself involved in a murder somewhere."

"I'm not asking you," I told him.

"That's all right, I'm telling you. I'm giving you a chance to come clean."

"I've come clean," I told him.

"All right," Sellers told me, "you've made your bed. You're the one that's going to have to lie in it. Don't say I didn't give you a chance. And I'll tell you right now, Lam, that if you tell me the truth, I'll do everything I can to substantiate your story. If it turns out you're telling the truth, I'll back you up all the way."

"I've told you the truth. Go ahead and try to substantiate it."

Sellers said, "Okay, if that's the way you want it. Don't try to leave town. I'll be wanting you for questioning tomorrow. Right now, you're mixed up in a murder case up to your eyebrows. Now, pull in to the curb."

Sellers signaled one of the police cars that was following,

walked over to it and got in. The police car swept into motion and went places fast.

As nearly as I could tell, I was on my own, no one was following me. I had a lot of things to do before daylight and very little time in which to do them.

Chapter 16

THE SKYVIEW MOTEL was down Santa Monica way.

At this hour of the night there was very little traffic. The lights were mostly out. The motel had a big red sign, SKYVIEW, and underneath it, a smaller sign, *Vacancy*.

I stopped the car and went up the stairs to the building with a sign on the door marked *Office*.

I pressed the night bell.

For twenty or thirty seconds nothing happened.

I pressed the bell again.

A light came on inside the office. A man's sleepy voice said, "All right."

After a moment, I saw a moving shadow, then a man pulling suspenders over his shoulders. He zipped up his pants and stumbled sleepily into the light.

"Got a single?" I asked.

"One left," he said.

"How much?"

"Six bucks."

I gave him the six dollars. He handed me a registration card and I filled it out, scrawling my signature.

"What's the license number of the car?" he asked.

"Oh, put down anything," I said.

"Nothing doing," he said. "I keep the license numbers. We had a little trouble here a few nights ago, and it's a damned good thing I had the license number."

I said, "I've forgotten what it is. Just a minute and I'll take a look."

"I'll check," he said.

He followed me out and made a note of the license number of the agency car.

I said, "What was the trouble?"

"Oh, nothing much," he said.

I said, "Are you referring to the man who had the heart attack here?"

"How did you know about it?"

I said, "I'm investigating it."

"What the hell! I thought you wanted a cabin."

"I did want a cabin," I told him. "That's why I'm here. I've given you the money. You give me the key. That's all there is to it. Now then, I am just asking you a few things about what happened."

"Look, buddy, I've told what happened."

"I know. I want you to tell again."

"Who are you?"

I opened the leather folder and flashed my I.D. card at him. "I'm an investigator," I said.

"Okay, okay, what do you want to know?"

I said, "Tell me what happened."

"There's nothing to it," he said. "This fellow drove up and registered—"

"About what time?"

"I don't know. Around nine o'clock, I guess—maybe nine-thirty."

"All right, he registered. . . . How did he register?"

"Under his own name, of course. He was a respectable guy. Baxter C. Gillett and wife."

"And the car he was driving?"

"He was driving a Cadillac. I went out on the porch to check the license number. I usually do that."

"Did you see the woman?"

"Only vaguely— Well, as a matter of fact, no, I didn't see her to get a good look at her. I just saw somebody in the car with him. I run a respectable place, but I'm not nosy. You can't run a motel if you ask to see the marriage certificate of every couple that registers."

"When did you first know there was anything wrong?"

"When the wife called me in the morning."

"What time?"

"About seven o'clock, I guess."

"And what happened?"

"She was almost hysterical, she wanted a doctor, she said her husband was sick, and then she said she thought he'd died during the night, and when she woke up, he was lying there dead."

"What did you do?"

"I went over and took a look. I could see the guy was dead as soon as I looked at him, but I helped her call a doctor, and then the doctor suggested we call the undertaker and the coroner's office—tried to hush it up as much as I could. That kind of stuff doesn't do a motel any good."

"What else?" I asked.

"That's all," he said.

"This was the night of the fourth?"

"That's right. That's when he died, I guess. She called me the morning of the fifth."

"After you rent your last cabin, you go to sleep?"

"I go to sleep before then. Sometimes I don't rent them all. Usually I roll in about ten or ten-thirty, but most of the time I sleep with one eye open."

"Notice anything unusual that night?" I asked. "Did anything out of the ordinary happen?"

"Nothing. Why?"

"I was just wondering," I said. "How about a taxicab? Did anyone come in a taxicab?"

He looked at me curiously. "Why do you ask that question?"

"Because I'm trying to get things straight in my own mind."

He said, "It's funny you should ask that question."

"Why?"

"Because," he said, "I— Well, like I said, I usually sleep with one eye open. That is, the first part of the night. Sometimes along toward the last part of the night I get into a pretty sound sleep."

139

"And this particular time?" I asked.

"Well," he said, "I was sort of sleeping with one eye open. A car drove in and I was dozing, sort of waiting for the bell to ring, and it didn't ring. I went back to sleep and then woke up and wondered why the bell hadn't rung, and went back to sleep again . . . just sort of dozing. You know the feeling you get. Maybe you're only sleeping twenty or thirty seconds at a time, but you're just sort of waiting for something to happen."

"All right, what happened?"

"That's the strange part of it. Nothing happened. So I settled down again, and then, after maybe four or five minutes, I came up wide-awake and thought it was sure funny that a car drove in and nobody rang the bell, because before I went to bed I'd checked and all the cabins that were occupied had the cars parked in front of them. So I started to get up, and when I did, this car came back out— That is, I presume it was the same car, and it was a taxicab."

"It didn't stop?"

"No, it went tearing right on through."

"You checked to see where it had been?"

"There was no way of checking. I looked out and the cabins were all dark and—"

"What time was it?"

"Around eleven, I guess. I'd been in bed for about an hour. I didn't look at the time."

"Then what happened?"

"Well, then I went to sleep and slept pretty sound. I had rented all the cabins that night and everything was full up, so there was nothing to keep me awake."

"Could another car have driven in without you hearing it?"

"Hell, yes. A dozen of them could have. After I get things all rented, I sleep a lot sounder than when I'm sort of half expecting to be called and have to get up and rent another cabin."

I said, "I suppose you read the account in the paper about Gillett having been found dead?"

"Sure, sure," he said, "of course I would. Why wouldn't I? When something happens that concerns you, you naturally watch for the account in the paper."

"You saw his picture?"

"Yes."

"A good likeness?"

"Hell, I don't know," he said. "I can't remember too much about the different people I rent cabins to. You see a whole procession of new faces night after night. I will say this, the picture was not too good. Usually those pictures they have in the obituary column are the kind that flatter a guy. This picture didn't flatter him—made him look a little older, I think."

"You saw his face when you went in the cabin, when he was lying there dead?"

"Just got a look at his profile. I didn't pay too much attention to his face. One arm was out and I started to feel for a pulse, but as soon as I touched him I knew he'd been dead for quite a while. He was stiff and getting pretty cool to the touch."

"Now look, Lam, I've told you everything I know. I've been over this a dozen times. What's your angle?"

"I'm just checking," I said. "Thanks a lot, Mr.— What was the name?"

"Fallon," he said, "Herbie Fallon."

"Your wife work here with you?"

"Nope. My wife died a year ago and I've been running the place on my own."

"Okay," I told him. "Thanks."

I rolled into bed but it was an hour before I could get to sleep. That motel, however, was the safest place I could be.

Chapter 17

I WAS UP with the first crack of dawn. I went to an all-night restaurant, had breakfast, three cups of coffee, then called Bertha Cool.

"What the hell are you calling me for at this hour of the morning?" she asked.

"Because I need your help."

"Look, Donald," she said, "you're in bad."

"I know I'm in bad."

"Sellers thinks you're mixed up in that murder. He isn't going overboard on it yet, because he doesn't want to have to back up. But he tells me you're in one hell of a mess. What the hell were you doing out there parked in the agency car and giving signals to that little minx?"

I said, "I want to talk to you about that, and I need your help."

"All right," she said, "you need my help. You've got me up at this ungodly hour, so you may as well get it over with. What do you want me to do?"

"I want you to meet me in front of the Vector Apartments."

"When?"

"In half an hour."

"My God, Donald, have a heart. I need coffee and—"

"Have coffee," I said, "but no breakfast. We may not have time."

"What do you want me to do when I get there?"

"I want you as a witness," I said.

"A witness to what?"

"Something important," I told her. "Will you be there?"

Bertha groaned and said, "All right, I'll be there."

Bertha Cool met me promptly at seven-thirty in front of the Vector Apartments.

I said, "Good morning, Bertha."

She glowered at me and said, "Good morning my fanny! You know damned well that I'm a bitch until I've had my three cups of coffee."

"Didn't you get them this morning?"

"I grabbed a cup of coffee on the run, but I feel like biting somebody's head off."

"Fine," I said, "that's the way you should feel."

"What do you want me to do?"

I said, "I'm going to talk with a woman. I think she's a very beautiful woman. I think she'll probably try to use sex and charm and all of the wiles of which she's capable."

"Well, if she uses any wiles on me, I'll slap her to sleep, Bertha said.

"Now, that's just the point," I told her. "I want you to keep in the background, get over, out of the line of fire, so to speak, and sit and watch. And if you come to the conclusion that she's lying and is trying to use sex appeal to sugar-coat a bunch of lies, then you can go to work. If you think she's telling the truth, then you just continue to sit there as a witness."

"All right," Bertha said, "Let's get this over with. I want to get some fried eggs, some hashed brown potatoes, half a dozen sausages and a quart pot of coffee."

"Okay," I told her. "Remember, keep in the background until you've reached a decision."

We went up in the elevator and I rang the chimes on Pauline Garson's apartment.

It was the third ring before I got any action. Then a sleepy voice said, "Yes, what is it?"

I said, "Something very important. We have to see you right away."

"Who are you?"

I said, "I'm Donald Lam, an investigator, that—"

"Oh, yes, Marilyn told me about you. She says you're nice. What is it you want, Mr. Lam?"

I said, "I simply have to talk with you right away."

"Well, I'm not decent and the apartment is a mess."

I said, "I *could* wait out here for a few minutes, but not long. It is a matter which won't wait."

"All right," she said, "give me five minutes."

We waited out in the corridor for about seven minutes. Bertha kept looking at her diamond-studded wrist watch and glowering at me with eyes that were as hard as the diamonds on her hand.

The young woman who opened the door was attired in a housecoat with a side zipper opening. She had on stockings and shoes, her hair was neatly combed, there was eye shadow tastefully applied and her mouth had been carefully made up.

She batted long eyelashes at me and said, "Good morning, Mr. Lam. I'm sorry that I— Who's this?"

"This," I said, "is Bertha Cool, my partner. This is Pauline Garson, Bertha."

Bertha grunted.

Pauline said, "Come in."

Bertha following instructions, moved over to a corner of the room and made herself as inconspicuous as possible.

Pauline sat in a straight-backed chair and indicated an overstuffed easy chair for me.

Morning light filtering through rose-colored shades softened her face and gave her a naïve, childlike appearance.

She adjusted the housecoat carefully.

After a moment, the housecoat slipped on the smooth silk of her stocking and showed lots of leg.

"All right, Donald," she said, "after all, I feel that I know you very well, indeed. Marilyn thinks you're wonderful. What is it?"

I said, "Let's go back to the night of the fourth."

"The fourth . . . the fourth," she said, frowning, and then laughed throatily. "Really, Donald, I'm not much good at going back on my night's activities, and I don't keep a diary."

I said, "You shouldn't have any difficulty remembering this

144

night, because you met a man from Santa Ana by the name of Baxter C. Gillett."

"Did I?" she asked, dimpling.

"You did."

"And then what happened?"

"You went out to dinner and someone was with you, probably you were on a foursome. The suggestion was made that you do a little dancing and drinking, and then something happened. Gillett wanted to terminate the evening, the relationship, and go home."

"Good heavens, Donald, you're talking about something that's entirely strange to me. Who in the world is this Baxter Gillett you're talking about?"

I said, "I don't know exactly the sequence of events, but afterwards Gillett was drugged and taken to the Skyview Motel down at Santa Monica.

"Then someone came and got you and took you to the motel. You went in the unit with Gillett and undressed, got into bed and—"

She straightened herself indignantly. "*I* undressed with a strange man in the room?"

I met her eyes. "You undressed with a strange man in the room."

She drew herself up with dignity and pulled the housecoat over the leg.

"Donald," she said, "I thought you were a gentleman. You disappoint me. You've made an accusation which is unfair and untrue. I'm afraid I'm going to have to ask you to leave."

I said, "You have been teamed up with Jeanette Latty. I don't know to what extent. You've made dates through her."

"Is that a crime?" she asked.

"It depends," I said.

"If you're going to try to pin anything on me," she said, "you're going to have to prove it."

"And," I said, "when Marilyn Chelan showed up, you remembered your association in Salt Lake City and got Marilyn a couple of dates. It soon turned out that Marilyn didn't enter into the spirit of things the way she was supposed to, but played things strictly according to the rules which were printed, rules that actually were so much eyewash, intended to surround the whole activity with an aura of respectability."

Pauline hesitated for a moment, then suddenly threw back her head and laughed.

The housecoat fell open once more. This time I could see well above the stocking.

"Donald," she said, "I *should* be mad at you, but there's something about the way you do things that makes you just downright charming.

"I'm going to tell you this much, Donald. I've been married and divorced and I know what it's all about, and I *did* take some dates through Jeanette Latty.

"Now, I don't know about the other girls, but I violated the rules."

She batted her eyes at me.

"After all, I'm a human being, Donald, and I have warm human emotions. If people appeal to me . . ." And here she batted her eyes at me again, "I'm inclined to get affectionate.

"But that's *all* I know. This Gillett business is all news to me.

"Now, I'm going to try to help you just as much as I can, because, frankly, Donald, *you* appeal to me. You have something that makes you— Well, I know you'd get mad if I said you were cute, but it's something that— Well, darn it, you are cute.

"Now, I *was* out on the night of the fourth with a four-some and—"

"And you saw Marilyn that night?"

"That's right. Marilyn was having dinner in the place where we ate. And then we went out for a drink at a night spot and my partner got a little conscience-stricken or something. He wanted to terminate the evening and get home, and— Well, he did."

"How?" I asked.

"He took me back to Jeanette Latty's and said good night."

146

"You went back to Jeanette Latty's?"

"Always," she said. "The deal was that everybody thought we lived at Jeanette Latty's house on Rhoda Avenue. They'd come there to get us and take us home there. We'd never invite them in except on very, very rare occasions. Jeanette Latty had a front room reserved for those occasions. But mostly we— Well, the evening was terminated before that. . . . We'd tell our dates that we were living there in a bungalow with our mother, that our mother was sickly and was in bed."

"Why?" I asked.

"Use your imagination," she said. "Jeanette was in business. She wanted to be able to check on us, and she didn't want us making dates on the side, on our own."

"What was the name of this man you were out with on the night of the fourth?"

"Heavens, Donald, I don't know. We would call each other by first names. I don't think his first name was Baxter. That would be a little hard to say. We never asked for last names. I might have called him by some pet name or some nickname, but I can't remember."

"And what did he call you?"

"They all called me the same. I told them I was Polly."

I said, "You're absolutely certain that you didn't go out again that night, after he took you back to Jeanette Latty's?"

"Of course, I'm certain," she said, dimpling at me. "Donald, I'm sorry I put on the act I did. After all, I'm no paragon of virtue and— Well, you're a man and you'll probably sense the way I feel toward men—I *like* them."

I glanced over at Bertha.

Bertha Cool sighed, got up from the chair, moved over to the center of the room and stood looking down at Pauline.

"So you like men, do you?"

"Yes."

Bertha said, "You're a god-damned little tart and you like money."

Pauline looked at her with her face going white and her jaw sagging.

I said, "For your information, Pauline, your friend, Baxter Gillett, was given some knock-out drops or some kind of a drug. It was an overdose and it killed him. You were in on the conspiracy and it ties you up with first-degree murder unless you come clean. Gillett was either given an overdose or his heart was weak and the drug brought on a heart attack."

"I don't know a thing in the world about it," Pauline said, trying to muster some dignity, "and I'm going to ask both of you to leave. Furthermore, Mrs. Cool, I am going to sue you for defamation of character. You have made remarks that are derogatory to my character and I don't have to sit here and take them."

"Go ahead and sue," Bertha said, "and I'll strip you naked in front of a jury. You little trollop, you've been putting on this act with Donald about his being so damned cute. As far as I'm concerned, you're just a god-damned overpriced call girl who likes money, and if you think you're going to hold out information on a murder, you've got another guess coming.

"*I'm* talking to you now. In about fifteen minutes, you're going to be talking to the cops—and don't slide that leg out at me. Start talking and start telling the truth."

"I have told you the truth. I am going to ask you to leave. Otherwise, I shall forcibly eject you."

"Forcibly eject me," Bertha said. "Start in."

Pauline made an ineffectual gesture to grab Bertha's shoulder.

Bertha grabbed her and threw her half across the room. The housecoat ripped off and left Pauline standing there with bra, panties and stockings.

"You wanted your legs to look good for Donald, so you didn't put on slippers, you put on high-heeled shoes," Bertha said. "Now, *I'm* going to tell *you* something, sister.

"You've got a sweet little racket. You've got a nice figure and you're peddling it. You're peddling it to a very select clientele, and you think you're sitting pretty. You've got a nice apartment here, you're wined and dined and you're doing all right for yourself.

"Now, how are you going to feel in prison, where you

wear a shapeless smock and flat-heeled sandals, where every dreary day is just like every other dreary day, with your youth and good looks and figure going down the drain, so that when you get out you'll be an old woman with a dumpy figure, no future ahead, but with a past that will rise up and hit you in the face every time you try to make an honest living.

"And they feed you starches instead of proteins in those prisons. You get fat and soft and flabby. You have to eat and what you eat is potatoes and bread and all that sort of crap.

"I'm talking about murder and prisons and police. I don't know who the hell is telling you to clam up on this thing, but whoever it is, is handing you a line of soft soap and you're staking your future—"

Pauline made a run for Bertha.

Bertha swung her right hand and caught Pauline in an open-handed smash across the face that sent her reeling.

Bertha followed up with a left.

"Go on, dearie," Bertha said, "get rough. I just love to have the party get rough. You god-damned lying little bitch. I'll slap you to sleep."

Pauline cowered in a corner.

"Start talking," Bertha said, glaring at her.

"You think you're being smart. You're just being the patsy, the fall guy. The people who are in on this racket are the ones who are smart. They're using you for bait and for merchandise, that's all. When the chips are down, they won't stand back of you for a damned minute. They'll just throw you to the wolves so they can save their own skins. You're just a female body to them—and there are lots more where you came from.

"For God's sake, haven't you been around enough to know the answers?"

Pauline started to say something and Bertha took a step forward.

Pauline threw up her hands in defense. "Don't," she said.

"Start talking," Bertha said, "and start making sense."

Pauline said, "It's . . . it's true."

"That's better," Bertha said. "Now, let's have the lowdown and have it fast, because we haven't got much time."

Pauline said, "I was given the job of warming this Baxter Gillett up, and we were supposed to— Well, the people who were running the thing wanted to have something on him."

"Who were the people?"

"I can't tell you their names, they'd kill me."

"Suppose I tell you their names," I said. "How about George Dix?"

"You know?" she asked.

Bertha said, "You damned little trollop. Get it through your head that Donald Lam knows the whole damned business, everything that happened, and the whole shooting works. Now, come through and come through clean."

She sat down and started to cry.

"Oh, for God's sake," Bertha said, "button that stuff up. Tears don't mean any more to me than nylon. I want facts."

Pauline said, "Well, you had it about right. They wanted something out of Gillett. I was to try and soften him up, and they wanted to get him in a spot. But he wouldn't go for it. So we said good night. Gillett drove away with George Dix. He was driving Gillett's car and they had a girl with them— George's girl. They left me at Jeanette's. And then, the next thing I knew, there was a telephone call and I was told to be ready to go places to spend the night."

"Where were you at the time?"

"I was sitting, talking with Jeanette Latty. She was a little peeved that the evening had busted up as early as it did and was inclined to intimate that I hadn't been properly co-operative."

"So what did you do?"

"Jeanette called a cab for me and—"

"Just a minute," I interrupted. "Who was the cabdriver, do you know?"

"Why, of course I know. It was Hermann. Hermann did just about all of Jeanette's work."

"All right, what happened?"

"Well, the cab took me down to this Skyview Motel and

I was told to go in unit fourteen, that my date was pretty drunk but that he had changed his mind and had become lonely, that he'd want companionship when he woke up."

"That was all they told you?"

"Yes."

"What did you do?"

"I got into bed with the guy. He was pretty far gone, so I started dozing off and then I heard him gasping and choking, and the next thing I knew, he was completely still. I thought he'd passed out and then I started listening to his heart, and there wasn't any heartbeat. I felt for his pulse and there was no pulse. I *knew* he was dead. I looked through his pockets and found a card with persons to notify in the event of accident, so I did what I thought was the square thing. I called his wife in Santa Ana and told her frankly that the guy was in a motel with me, that he had died and I was checking out."

"And what did she do?"

"I read about it in the paper. She was a real sport. She drove in, got into bed with him and then pretended to discover his death the next morning."

"Did you tell her where you'd leave the key?"

"Yes, under the mat."

Bertha said, "All right, dearie, get some clothes on. I'm sorry I slapped you so hard, but you put some cold compresses on your face and you'll be all right."

I walked over to the phone, picked it up and said, "I want to get Sergeant Frank Sellers at police headquarters. It's important."

Chapter 18

FRANK SELLERS was skeptical at first, but he listened to Pauline's story. His eyes narrowed to thoughtful slits. He kept chewing his cigar, rolling it around in his mouth and occasionally taking his eyes from Pauline to glance at Bertha and at me.

When Pauline had finished, he asked her a flock of questions, then turned to me. "All right, Pint Size," he said, "you're masterminding this game. I'm not buying anything yet. What's your idea of the next move?"

I said, "Hermann Oakley, the cabdriver."

"Oakley's okay. He's in the clear," he said. "He's been co-operating with the police. I know all about Oakley."

"Let's see if you do," I said.

"I tell you, he's told me the whole business," Sellers said. "He had a pretty shrewd idea what was going on out at Jeanette's, but as long as he was getting fares and tips, he kept his mouth shut."

"Did he tell you about that trip down to the motel in Santa Monica?" I asked.

"No," Sellers said, "he didn't." Then he added, after a moment, "And I didn't ask him. Of course, it's *your* idea that this guy had been drugged and there was a murder mixed up in it. My idea is, he kept thinking things over, decided he'd been a little too puritanical, had a couple of drinks and sent for the gal to come back and spend the night."

"All right," I said, "let's ask Hermann Oakley. If he's co-operating so readily with the police, he should corroborate Pauline's story."

"Suppose he does? Then what?"

"Let's see," I said.

Sellers said, "Dammit, Donald, you're always trying to

cut yourself a piece of cake. Now, you're mixed in this thing up to your neck. I don't know anything about this Gillett business. How the hell is anybody going to prove it was a murder? You say the guy had been given knockout drops. The coroner has signed it out as a natural death due to heart failure. The body's been cremated. No one can ever prove a damned thing."

I said, "Oakley was lying. I didn't give Marilyn Chelan any signals. I wasn't sitting there when she drove up in the cab. He's got his time element all wrong."

"The guy could be mistaken," Sellers said. "You, yourself, said there was another car the same make and model as yours cruising around out there. He could have seen that."

"That's right, he *could.*"

"And you *could* be lying."

"That's right," I told him. "Let's talk with Oakley."

Sellers sighed and got to his feet. "Okay," he said.

He turned to Pauline. "You sit tight," he said. "Don't talk with anybody. Don't talk with newspaper reporters. Don't ring up this guy, Dix. If the phone rings, don't answer it. If anybody knocks at the door, don't go to the door. Sit tight. Don't make any moves. Pretend you're not home. You stay put until I get back. When I get back, I'll ring your bell three times, wait a minute, then ring two times, wait a minute, then ring once. When you hear that signal, open the door. Until you hear that signal, sit tight, don't make a move."

Sellers moved wearily toward the door. "Come on, Pint Size."

Bertha said, "Do you need me? I'm famished. I want breakfast and—"

"We need you here," Sellers said. "Stick around."

"Do you have Oakley's address?" I asked. "I think he works nights."

"Of course I've got his address," Sellers said. "That's the trouble with you damned amateurs. You think the cops bungle *everything.* Come on, let's get the hell out of here and get it over with."

Sellers had a police cruiser waiting and we rode out to the place where Oakley lived.

The place was a run-down apartment district and Oakley had a room in a small apartment house that had a good-looking front on the outside but smelled of stale cooking odors on the inside.

Sellers found the right apartment and pounded on the door.

After a moment, a masculine, sleepy voice said, "What the hell?"

Sellers said, "This is Sergeant Sellers of the police. Open up."

"Oh, my God," the voice said, "I've told you all I know a dozen times over."

"I said open up," Sellers said.

Oakley was wide-awake now.

"Look," he protested, "it isn't convenient for me to have you come in here now, Sergeant. You go down and sit in your car. I'll dress and be down in two minutes."

Sellers said, "Open up."

"I'm . . . I'm not alone," Oakley said.

"Dammit," Sellers said, "I said open up."

After a moment, the door opened.

Oakley, with his hair tousled, was in pants and shirt. A good-looking babe was in the bed, with the covers pulled up to her chin, looking frightened half to death.

Sellers ignored the girl. He walked over and sat on the foot of the bed. I stood by the dresser.

Sellers said, "Let's go back to the night of the fourth. What about this business of you taking a babe down to a motel in Santa Monica?"

"Me?" Oakley asked, with an air of injured dignity.

"You," Sellers said.

"I don't have any independent recollection of it, Sergeant," Oakley said, and then looked at me. "What's he doing, trying to take the heat off himself by getting me in bad with the cops?"

"I'm asking the questions," Sellers said. "Did you take a babe down to the Skyview Motel?"

"I'd have to look up my worksheet to be sure, but . . ." Oakley squirmed.

"Hell, you wouldn't forget a deal like that," Sellers said. "Did you?"

"Well, I . . . I'll put it this way. I may have."

"Why didn't you tell me about it?"

"Tell you about it?" Oakley said. "What the hell does that have to do with the case you're investigating?"

"I don't know," Sellers said, "but I wanted to find out everything you knew about the activities of Jeanette Latty and the girls she used."

"Well, I told you."

"You didn't tell me about Pauline Garson," Sellers said.

"Pauline . . . I don't know any Pauline— Oh, do you mean Polly?"

"Perhaps I do. You didn't tell me about Polly."

"I didn't see too much of Polly," Oakley said. "There were quite a few other girls that— Well, they used to ask for me. You see, it's like I told you. Jeanette didn't want to have too much attention attracted to the place or the type of deal she was running, so she tried to concentrate all the business on one cabdriver. They'd always ask for me, and, if I was at liberty, why, the dispatcher would send me out. If I wasn't, they'd use one of the other cabs."

Sellers rolled his cigar around in his mouth, looked at the girl in the bed, and said, "Who's she?"

"A friend," Oakley said.

I opened the dresser drawer and rummaged around a bit.

"What's your name?" Sellers asked the girl.

"Dolly," she said.

"You one of Jeanette Latty's girls?" Sellers asked.

She hesitated a moment, then nodded.

"You didn't tell me about Dolly," Sellers said to Oakley.

"Dolly is a particular friend of mine," Oakey said. "I was trying to protect her."

"In other words, you held out on me?"

"As far as Dolly is concerned, yes."

"And Polly," Sellers said.

"All right, and Polly," Oakey said. "I may have slipped

up a little bit on the minor stuff, but, for the most part, I told you all I knew."

I reached in the drawer, pulled out a woman's woolen stocking and tossed it over to Sellers.

"This mean anything to you?" I asked.

Sellers looked at it for a minute, started to shake his head, then suddenly his attention was riveted to the peculiar pattern.

"Well, I'll be go to hell!" he said. "It's a mate to the stocking that had the rock in it that cracked Jeanette Latty over the head."

Hermann Oakley made a wild dive for the door.

Frank Sellers moved with the precision of a well-oiled machine. He held the stocking in his left hand, his right crossed over to Oakley's jaw and flattened him.

Sellers looked at the stocking again, looked at me, then pulled out his handcuffs, turned over the inanimate form of Hermann Oakley, snapped the handcuffs on his wrist and said to Dolly, "Okay, sister, get your clothes on."

"In front of all you people?" she asked.

Sellers looked at her in dour appraisal. "Don't make me laugh."

Dolly sighed and got out of bed.

Chapter 19

THE NEWSPAPERS played it up big.

Frank Sellers and the Captain of Detectives shared the credit for uncovering a complex crime with nothing to go on but a woman's woolen stocking with a rock in it.

They rehashed the murder of Jeanette Latty, told about her escort service on Rhoda Avenue, which was really a front for the criminal activities of Hermann Oakley, a taxi driver, and George Littleton Dix, a real estate promoter by day, a procurer and blackmailer by night.

156

They cautiously referred to Archer as "the socially prominent executive of a big importing firm" who was short in his accounts and had appealed to his friend, Dix, to help him out. Due to an impending proxy fight, they had wanted to control the corporation. Together, they had hatched up a scheme by which the executive's boss was to be caught in a compromising position. When the victim refused to fall for the scheme, the conspirators tried to cover their back trail.

Jeanette Latty, however, had learned enough about the scheme to try her own hand at a little blackmail, and since this threatened to bring down the whole house of cards, Dix and Oakley met with Jeanette Latty to force her back into line.

The quarrel was written up in detail. Oakley had hit the woman over the head with a blackjack made by putting a rock in a woolen stocking. Dix had strangled the unconscious woman. The business executive, who had been scheduled to meet with the pair, became alarmed when he thought the police were watching the house and had not been in on the murder meeting. Police were at present withholding his name but making an intensive investigation.

In covering their trail, the pair had tried to exert pressure on one of the girls who had seen too much, hoping to force her to leave town. This had given Sergeant Sellers a lead. He had confided in Captain of Detectives Donald Matheson, and these two veteran officers cracked the case within less than forty-eight hours of intensive 'round-the-clock' work.

As for Dix, he was still a fugitive from justice. Oakley had turned state's evidence, announced his intention of pleading guilty and throwing himself on the mercy of the court. Police felt that the executive of the importing company had not been in on the actual murder, nor had he been a partner in the business carried on by Jeanette Latty, Dix and the cab-driver, but he had tried to use the combination to help win a proxy fight.

Nothing was said about the death of Baxter C. Gillett.

"What about Gillett?" Bertha asked. "Will all this stuff come out?"

"No," I said. "I talked with Norman Clinton on the phone.

157

Police feel that Gillett was not interested in the bait they had planned to use. Instead, he called up his wife and they started on a vacation.

"The body's been cremated. There can't be any proof of poison. It's a cinch the murderers won't say anything about it, and the police don't dare to, because they can't prove a damned thing and they don't want it to appear a murder slipped through their fingers.

"As far as they're concerned, one crime at a time is all they want to cope with."

Bertha thought that over, looking at the paper.

Captain Matheson and Frank Sellers had their pictures all over the paper, and the Chief was reported to be planning a citation. The "fearless officers" had started on a clueless case and kept working day and night until they had solved it.

"All right," Bertha said at length, "you're a brainy little bastard. But what the hell is in all this for us?"

"I don't know," I told her. "At least we did a good job for a client."

"What client?" Bertha asked.

There was a timid knock at the door.

"Who is it?" Bertha called.

"Elsie Brand."

"Well, come on in, Elsie. Don't be so damned namby-pamby. What is it *this* time?"

Elsie Brand handed me a special delivery letter. "This just came for you, Donald," she said, "and it's marked urgent."

I tore it open. It was a check signed by Ruth C. Gillett for twenty-five hundred dollars.

There was no word of explanation.

I tossed it on Bertha's desk.

"We might begin with that," I said.

Bertha looked at it and said softly, "Fry me for an oyster! You sure as hell do get the women."

Elsie still stood there.

"Well," Bertha said, "is there anything else?"

"Marilyn Chelan is in the office," Elsie said. "She wants

to thank Donald and wants to see him in person in order to do it."

Bertha's greedy hands grabbed the check. She picked up a rubber stamp endorsement, slammed it down on the inked pad, banged it on the back of the check, handed it to Elsie and said, "All right, take this down and deposit it, and let Marilyn thank Donald. But be sure the bastard wipes off the lipstick before any more clients come in."

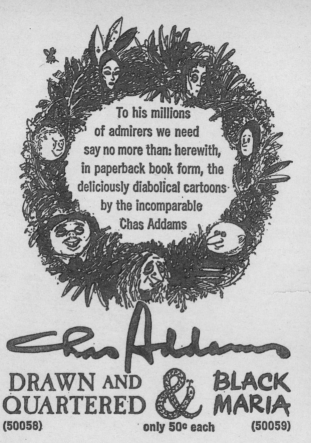